"Vladimir Sorokin [is] Russia's most inventive contemporary author."
—Masha Gessen, *The New York Times Book Review*

"Vladimir Sorokin, the translatosphere's favorite contemporary Russian novelist, writes about, and with the pitilessness of, his country's unremitting cold . . . *The Blizzard* . . . is a crazed fantasia on Tolstoy's tale, with all the moralizing ingeniously whited out."
—Joshua Cohen, *Harper's*

"*Day of the Oprichnik* is Vladimir Sorokin's funniest and most accessible book since *The Queue*. The KGB orgy scene at the end is worthy of the great shit-eating scenes of his earlier work."
—Keith Gessen, author of *All the Sad Young Literary Men*

"So we yearn for certainty, salvation, the absolute—what's wrong with that? We always have and we always will. Go ahead, Sorokin seems to say; you can't really help it. Just be careful what you wish for . . . Those readers (and reviewers) who turn to literature for consolation, or moral enlightenment, or lessons in self-esteem, are well advised to look elsewhere."
—Christian Caryl, *The New York Review of Books*

"Sorokin's novel packs a hefty satirical punch that will show American audiences why the author has been so controversial in Russia . . . Great fun, with a wickedly absurdist humor that occasionally reminds one of William S. Burroughs."
—*Booklist*

OTHER BOOKS BY VLADIMIR SOROKIN IN ENGLISH TRANSLATION

The Blizzard

Day of the Oprichnik

Ice Trilogy

The Queue

Telluria

THEIR FOUR HEARTS

Vladimir Sorokin

Translated from the Russian by Max Lawton

Dalkey Archive Press
Dallas/Dublin

Originally published in Russia as *Сердца четырёх* by Конец Века
Copyright © 1994 by Vladimir Sorokin
Translation © 2022 by Max Lawton

Paperback: 9781628973969
Ebook: 9781628974126

Library of Congress Control Number: 2022931025

Exterior design by Alban Fischer
Artwork © 2022 by Gregory Klassen
Artwork photography by Patrick Grandaw: grandawcreative.com
www.dalkeyarchive.com
Dallas/Dublin

Their Four Hearts

Vladimir Sorokin unleashed a gruesome
parade of atrocities into the world with his
1995 novel

СЕРДЦА ЧЕТЫРЁХ
(Their Four Hearts)

mere English being insufficient translation

I have rectangled these
horrors with charcaol on paper

OLEG OPENED THE DOOR WITH HIS FOOT and walked into the bakery. It was nearly empty. He walked over to the shelf and grabbed two twenty-kopeck loaves of white bread and a half loaf of black bread. Got in line behind a woman. Soon, he was at the front of the line.

"Fifty kopecks," said the grey-haired cashier.

Oleg gave her a ruble.

"Your fifty kopecks," the cashier handed them back to him.

Pressing the bread to his chest, he walked over to the exit. Walking through the door, he pulled out a plastic bag and began to stick the bread into it. One loaf fell out of his hands and into a puddle.

"Damn . . ." Oleg bent over and picked up the loaf. It was dirty and wet. Oleg walked over to a trash can and dropped the loaf into it. He shifted the bag into a more comfortable position and set off home.

"Hey, young man, hold on!" someone called out from behind him.

Oleg looked back. A tall old man walked up to him, leaning on to his cane. He wore a tattered grey coat and an army ushanka hat. In his left hand, the old man was holding a string bag with a black loaf in it. The old man's face was thin and calm.

"Hold on," the old man repeated, "what's your name?"

"Me? Oleg," responded Oleg.

Oleg opened the door with his foot and walked into the bakery. It was nearly empty. He walked over to the shelf and grabbed two twenty-kopeck loaves of white bread and a half loaf of black bread. Got in line behind a woman. Soon, he was at the front of the line.

"And my name is Henry Ivanych. Tell me, Oleg, are you in a great hurry?"

"No, not really."

The old man nodded.

"Good. You probably live in that tower block over there. Am I right?"

"You guessed it," grinned Oleg.

"Very good. I live a little further away. By Ocean, y'know, the sea-food store," the old man smiled. "I tell you what Oleg, if you're not in any rush, let's start to walk along our, so to speak, common path and have a chat. I have something to discuss with you."

They set off side by side.

"You know what I can't stand most in this world, Oleg? It's when people get preachy. I've never respected people who do that. I remember, before the war, I went away to a Young Pioneer camp one summer. Our counselor turned out to be a terrible moralist. He told us kids how we had to be. Putting it briefly, I had to get out of there . . ."

The old man walked quietly for a little while, his prosthesis creaking as he stared at his feet. Then he started to talk again.

"When the war began, I'd just turned fourteen. How old are you?"

"Thirteen," Oleg responded.

"Thirteen," the old man repeated. "Have you heard of the Siege of Leningrad?"

"I've heard of it . . ."

"You've heard of it . . ." the old man repeated. He sighed, then began talking again. "I lived with my grandma and my little sister Verochka back then. My father was killed on the first day of the war—June 22nd— in Belarus, near Brest. My older brother was killed near Kharkov. My mother too, in a bomb shelter on Vasilyevsky Island. And only we remained: the oldest and the youngest. Grandma got work at a hospital, she took Verochka along on her shifts, and I got a job at a factory. They taught me grown-up work, Oleg: putting together shells for Katyusha

"Let's start to walk along our, so to speak, common path and have a chat."

rocket launchers. In two and a half years, I put together enough to knock out a whole division of fascists. Yep. If the people in charge hadn't been so rotten, that Zhdanov first among 'em, our city would've led a normal life. But the bastards had their heads up their asses and they shoved us right up there with 'em: they didn't do anything to protect the food-stuffs, they couldn't save 'em. The Germans bombed the Badayevsky warehouses, they burned, and us boys just laughed. We didn't know what was coming. Everything burned: flour, butter, sugar . . . Then, in the winter, women went to where the warehouses'd been, dug up dirt, boiled it, and filtered it. They say that this made a sweet broth. 'Cause of the sugar. Anyways, the ration was 200 grams of bread for those who worked and 125 grams for those who didn't. When Lake Ladoga froze, we sent Verochka to the mainland on the 'Road of Life.' I sat her in the truck myself. Granny crossed herself and wept: 'at least she'll survive.' And then, when the siege ended, I found out that Verochka didn't make it. The Germans flew down and put six trucks of wounded people and children under the ice . . ."

The old man stopped and pulled out a crumpled handkerchief. Blew his nose.

"Yes, Oleg, that's how things were. But I wanted to tell you about one event in particular. It was the second winter of the siege. The most difficult time. It's possible that I made it through only because I was a kid. Granny died. The neighbors died. And not just them. Every morning, someone got taken away on a sled. And I was working at the factory. I would go into the foundry, warm up. Then make my way to my spot on the assembly line. Yep. And on New Year's Eve, one of my father's colleagues visited me. Vasily Nikolaevich Koshelyov. He would come by from time to time and bring canned food or grains. He helped me bury Granny. He comes over and says, 'come on, Stakhanovite, get dressed.' 'Where to?' I ask. 'A secret,' he says, 'a New Year's present.' I get dressed. We go. He takes me to the bread factory. He led me through the entrance. And into his office. He was the secretary of the party committee there. He locks the door. Opens the safe and pulls out sliced bread and a can of tushonka. He pours me hot water with saccharine. 'Eat, Stakhanovite' he says, 'Don't rush.' I attack the bread and the tushonka. And this bread, Oleg, you probably wouldn't even eat this bread. It was as black as chernozem, heavy, and wet. At that moment, though, it was sweeter to me than any cake. I ate everything, drank the boiling-hot water, and became just intoxicated, I fell down and couldn't get up. Vasily Nikolaich picked me up and lay me down on a mattress near the radiator. 'Sleep till morning,' he says. He worked next to me all day and night. I was dead to the world, he woke me up in the morning. Fed me again, but a little bit less this time. 'And now,' he says, 'let's go, I want to show you our enterprise.' He led me through the workshops. I saw thousands of loaves. Thousands. They were floating through the room on a conveyor belt like in a dream. I'll never forget it. Then he took me into the pantry. In the pantry was a box. A box filled with bread crumbs. They would put the box at the end of the conveyor belt and crumbs would fall into it, you see. Yep. Vasily Nikolaich took a scoop and poured 'em into my boots. The crumbs just kept coming. Then he says, 'Happy New Year, Defender of Leningrad. Set off home, don't loiter around.' And I left. I'm walking through the city, snow, drifts, ruined buildings. The crumbs crunch in my boots. So warm. Nice. I made those crumbs last for a whole week. I ate 'em little by little. If I survived, it's because he put those crumbs into my boots. That, Oleg, is the whole story. And this is your building," the old man indicated the tower block with his cane.

Oleg was silent. The old man adjusted his ushanka and coughed.

"And that's the thing, Oleg. It just came back to me now. When you dropped the loaf of white bread into the trash can, I remembered those crumbs. My grandmother stiff with cold. Our dead neighbors swollen with hunger. I remembered and thought, 'goddamn, life's a crazy thing.' Back then, I was praying for crumbs and hunting for rats, but here, now, they're throwing loaves of white bread into trash cans. It's funny and it's sad. What was the point of all our suffering? What was the point of all those deaths?"

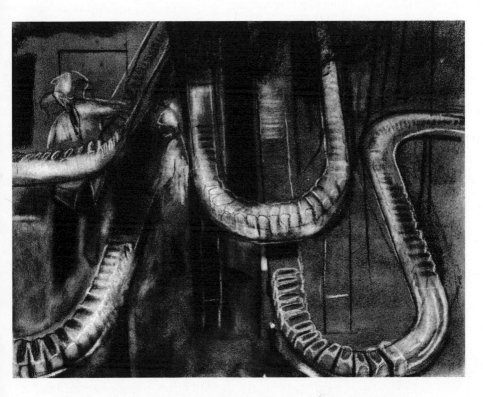

"He led me through the workshops. I saw thousands of loaves of bread. Thousands. They were floating through the room on a conveyor belt like a dream."

He was silent.

Oleg slowed down a bit, then said, "Well . . . you know. I . . . This . . . Actually . . . Nothing like that will ever happen again."

"Is that so?" the old man smiled sadly.

"Mhmm."

"You promise?"

"I promise."

"Well thank God. I have to admit I was worried when I started talking to you. I thought, 'this young man will listen a little, listen just a little, and then run away from the old fart, run away like I ran away from the Young Pioneer camp!' "

"Of course not—don't be silly. I understand. It's . . . it was stupid, I guess. I'll never throw bread away again."

"That's terrific. I don't know about everyone else, but I believe in your generation. *You* will save Russia. I'm sure of it. I hope I'm not detaining you?"

"Of course not—don't be silly."

"In that case, would you mind walking me home? It's right over there."

"Of course I'll walk you home. Let me carry your bag."

"Why thank you," the old man handed him the string bag with the bread in it, put his now free hand onto Oleg's shoulder, and they began to walk.

"Where were you wounded?" asked Oleg.

"My leg? That's another story. A long one too, enough for a whole novel . . . But enough of the heavy stuff. What grade're you in?"

"In sixth grade. At that school over there."

"Mmm. How do you like it?"

"It's okay."

"Do you have good friends?"

"I do."

"And girlfriends?"

Oleg shrugged and smirked.

"You know, it's time you started feeling like a man. At your age, you have to learn how to chase after girls. And in, say, a year and a half, you'll be able to fuck. Or will that be too early, do you think?"

"No, no," Oleg laughed, "I don't think so."

"That's right. I didn't think so either. You know how many girls, how many women, were left without husbands after the siege? You're walking down Nevsky and, oh, how they would stare at you! Enticingly. Once I went to the cinema. The first cinema to open up after the siege. They were showing *Alexander Nevsky*. There was a woman sitting next to me. Suddenly, in the middle of the movie, I realize she has her hand on my leg. I don't do anything. She unbuttons my pants and grabs my cock. She was trembling so much. I just sat there. She bent over and started to suck my cock. Do you know how nice that feels? I came in her mouth right away. And on screen—the Battle on the Ice! And she whispers to me, 'let's go to mine.' So, we went to hers. On Liteyny. We fucked all day and night. There was nothing she wouldn't do with me! She could suck a cock like nobody else. So, so tenderly, a moment passes, a moment, and already I'm coming. Has anyone ever sucked your cock?"

"No," Oleg shook his head.

"That's just fine—everything lies ahead. We've arrived!" The old man stopped outside of a five-story prefab building. "And here lies my village, here lies my native land. Thank you for walking with me."

"You're very welcome," Oleg gave the old man his string bag.

"Aha! And what's going on over here?" the old man pointed his cane at a green construction trailer that was standing beneath the trees next to his building. The door of the trailer was ajar. "Old freebooter that I am, I can't pass by without investigating! Follow me, boy!" He waved his string bag and limped over to the trailer.

Oleg followed.

"The door's open, there's no lock, and the light's been extinguished. It would seem that redskins've been here!"

"I came in her mouth right away. And on screen—the Battle on the Ice!"

They approached the trailer. The old man walked up the stairs and went inside. He felt for the light switch and flipped it.

"Aha. No light. Follow me, Oleg."

Oleg walked in behind him. It was cramped inside the trailer. It smelled of paint and feces. A streetlight shined in from outside, illuminating table, chairs, boxes, cans of paint, and rags.

"Here we are," the old man muttered, before suddenly throwing his cane and string bag off to the side and getting down onto his knee in front of Oleg, his prosthesis jutting out awkwardly. His hands grabbed Oleg's hands. "Oleg! Please listen to me, my dear . . . I'm an old, unhappy man, disabled by war and labor . . . My dear . . . My only joys are bread and margarine . . . Oleg, my sweet boy, I'm asking you to let me to suck you off. For the love of Christ, my dear, let me do it!"

Oleg backed over to the door, but the old man held on to his hands tenaciously.

"It'll be so nice for you, my sweet, sweet boy, it'll be so tender . . . You'll understand immediately . . . And you'll learn a bit so that it'll be easier with girls, let me do it, my dear, just for a little while . . . It won't take long. I'll give you a tenner, here, a tenner!"

The old man reached into his pocket and pulled out a stack of paper money.

"Here, here, my dear, ten, twenty, twenty-five! For the love of Christ!"

"Um . . ." Oleg wrenched his hands free and managed to run out the door, knocking a tray of cigarette butts off of the table as he did.

Having lost his balance, the old man fell down onto the floor and lay there for a little while, sobbing and muttering to himself.

Suddenly, the figure of a young boy appeared in the door.

"Oleg! I'm begging you!" the old man twitched.

"I'm not Oleg," the boy responded quietly, entering the room.

"Seryozha? You're following me, you're following me . . . Oh God . . ."

"I'm going to tell Rebrov everything, Henry Ivanych," the boy pronounced, closing the door.

"Bastard, such a bastard . . ." the old man began to turn and push himself up, "bastards, bitches . . . My God, such pigs . . ."

The boy walked over to the window and stood there, staring down at the old man. The old man located his cane, gathered his money, and, getting up onto his knees, stuffed the money into his coat pocket.

"Everyone's against me. Everyone and everything. My God, I'm not a clown . . ."

"You signed the contract," the boy spoke up, "but you're at it again . . ."

"Seryozha . . . Seryozha!" The old man crawled over to him, grabbed on to his legs, and pressed his face to his jacket. "These heartless . . . people . . ."

Suddenly he pulled away and almost screamed, "You know what . . . don't try to teach me, you bastard!"

"I have nothing to teach you. Rebrov will teach you."

"I don't give a shit! I don't give a shit!" the old man quaked. "I piss and I shit on you! Piss and shit! You pigs! I'm the responsible one! Me!"

"We're all responsible . . ." the boy looked out the window.

"You know what, Seryozha," the old man pronounced sternly. "Don't you dare contradict me!"

"I'm not contradicting you," the boy breathed onto the window and wiped away the fog with his finger.

"Well then," the old man started to unbutton the boy's pants.

The boy sighed unhappily and began to help him. Grabbing the boy by his exposed buttocks, the old man tongued his tiny penis into his mouth and froze, moaning. Seryozha breathed onto the glass and drew a swastika in the fog. The old man moaned. His sinewy fingers kneaded the boy's buttocks. The boy grabbed on to the old man's head and began to help him by moving his hips. The old man moaned louder. His awkwardly protruding prosthesis trembled, hitting the table leg. The boy closed his eyes. His lips parted.

"Tightly," he said.

The old man began to low.

"Tightly, tightly . . ." whispered Seryozha. "Tightly . . . ooh . . . tightly . . ."

The old man moaned. The boy shuddered twice and stopped moving. The old man let him go, leaned back, and began to breathe in greedily, sobbing now.

"Ah . . . Ah . . . so sweet . . . ah . . ." the old man mumbled. The boy bent over and pulled up his pants. "Ooh . . . Divine nectar . . . so little . . ." the old man kissed the boy's penis, wiped his own lips, and stood up from the floor heavily.

Seryozha buttoned up, fixed his jacket, and pulled a watch on a chain out of his pocket.

"Three minutes to seven."

"Motherfucker . . . right, right now . . . ugh . . ." the old man leaned against the boxes and clutched at his chest. "Let me take a breath . . . oof . . ."

"And the gas? You didn't forget it?" asked Seryozha.

"Everything . . . everything's in order . . . oy. I stood up so suddenly and my head just . . . oof . . . Let's go . . ." The old man pushed himself off of the boxes, went out the door, and began to walk down the steps cautiously.

"What about the bread, Henry Ivanych?" As he was leaving, Seryozha had noticed the bag of bread.

"Fuck the bread," the old man muttered.

The old man rang the doorbell: three short rings, one long. The door immediately opened and he and Seryozha went in.

"What's the meaning of this, Henry Ivanych?" Rebrov asked, locking the door with a chain. "Seryozha?"

"The meaning, the meaning," the old man muttered to himself, unbuttoning his coat. "The meaning is that I'm not thirty-five, but sixty-six . . ."

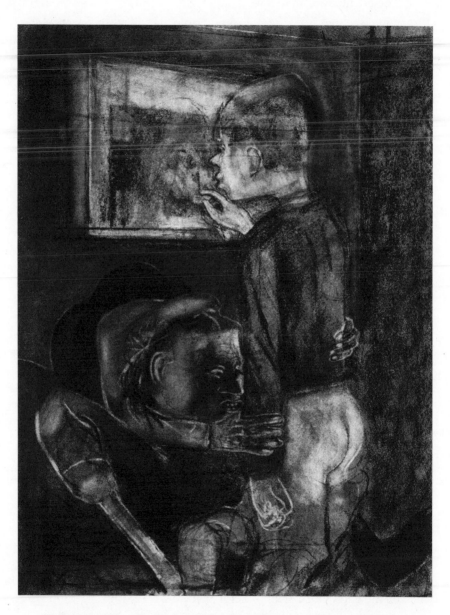

"Tightly, tightly . . ." whispered Seryozha. "Tightly . . . ooh . . . tightly . . ."

"It's still rush hour, Viktor Valentinych," Seryozha took off his hat and threw it onto a coat hanger.

"Twenty minutes! How is this acceptable?" Rebrov helped the old man to take off his jacket.

"It's really, truly not a big deal," the old man mumbled, taking off his galoshes with the end of his cane.

They walked down the hallway and entered a large, empty room. Pestretsova was sitting on the windowsill and smoking.

"Shtaube, my darling! Seryozhenka!" She jumped up, ran over, and kissed both of them.

"Welcome, Olga Vladimirovna, welcome," the old man laughed.

"Olka!" the boy smiled.

"You naughty boys!" she laughed.

"Breaking rules is sad, my friends. It's not funny," Rebrov bent over an open suitcase. "If this tardiness is going to set the tone for our enterprise, I can just cut loose. Someone special's waiting for me in Kiev."

"Don't exaggerate, Vitya," Pestretsova dropped her cigarette onto the ground and pressed it down with her boot. "We've still got reams of time."

"Yes and what . . . what, in fact, is the rush? I mean, is the train leaving?" Shtaube looked into the suitcase. "Oy yoi yoi . . . You haven't wasted any time, Viktor Valentinovich."

The suitcase was filled with various instruments, metallic components, blocks, and plates.

"No, I haven't," Rebrov pulled out a hammer and a broad chisel with a plexiglass handle and laid them both down on the floor. "Do you have the gas cartridges?"

"I do," Shtaube reached into his pocket.

"Hold on to them for now," Rebrov closed the suitcase and stood up. "So. Please pay attention."

He walked over to the window, pulled the dirty curtains more tightly shut, turned around, and began to speak, rubbing his hands together.

"So. For your information, we will not be conducting Operation No. 1 today, but Pre-Operation No. 1. Accordingly, the inclined series, the capitalistic, and the brightlight shall all be reduced. Let's begin."

Everyone began to undress, putting their clothes down onto the floor.

Pestretsova helped the old man to remove his prosthesis from its stump. Rebrov, now naked, walked over to the cube in the corner of the room. The cube was built from thick plywood and four leather straps were attached to one of its sides. Rebrov knelt down, put his arms through the straps, and stood up, the cube resting on his back.

Olga and Seryozha led Shtaube over to the cube.

"The lid," Rebrov ordered.

Olga removed the top of the cube and laid it down onto the floor. Then, she and Seryozha helped Shtaube to fit his naked body into the cube.

"There . . ." Shtaube muttered from inside the cube.

Olga put the lid back onto the cube, completely enclosing Shtaube. Seryozha gave her the hammer and four nails. She inserted the nails into the four apertures at the corners of the cube's lid and nailed it down.

"How is it?" a muffled voice came from the cube.

"I'm managing," replied Rebrov, spreading his legs further apart.

Olga lay facedown between his legs. Seryozha lay down on top of Olga, his back resting on hers.

"There!" Rebrov loudly pronounced.

Shtaube coughed and began to speak.

"54, 18, 76, 92, 31, 72, 72, 82, 35, 41, 87, 55, 81, 44, 49, 38, 55, 55, 31, 84, 46, 54, 21, 13, 78, 19, 63, 20, 76, 42, 71, 39, 86, 24, 91, 23, 17, 11, 73, 82, 18, 68, 93, 44, 72, 13, 22, 58, 72, 91, 83, 24, 66, 71, 62, 82, 12, 74, 48, 55, 81, 24, 83, 77, 62, 72, 29, 33, 71, 99, 26, 83, 32, 94, 57, 44, 64, 21, 78, 42, 98, 53, 55, 72, 21, 15, 76, 18, 18, 44, 69, 72, 98, 20."

Then, Olga began to speak.

"Ste, ipu, aro, ste, chae, poi, ste, goy, uva, ste, ogo, ano, ste, zae, heu, ste, acha, loe, ste, eje, iti, ste, avu, ene, olo, ste, odo, ave, ste, ije, aja, ste, uko, lao, ste, shuya, sai, ste, nae, yako, ste, dia, sae, ste, ira, sio, ste, yava, yuko, ste, zao, myo, ste, huo, dia, ste."

After Olga, Seryozha began to speak.

"Indigo, indigo, yellow, orange, indigo, red, green, green, yellow, purple, blue, red, green, purple, yellow, blue, indigo, green, orange, orange, red, purple, yellow, yellow, indigo, blue, red, green, indigo, purple, blue, orange, orange."

Then Rebrov began to sing.

"Sol, do, fa, fa, sol, mi, re, la, fa, fa, ti, sol, do, do, ti, sol, fa, re, la, la, mi, ti, do, re, re, fa, sol, ti, la, do, la, fa, sol, mi, fa, la, la, do, re, mi, ti, fa, la, sol, re, mi, la, do, mi, la, la, sol, do, fa, la, ti, re, do, ti, ti, re, fa, mi, ti, do, sol, sol, do, fa, la, ti, mi, mi, la, re, do, mi, ti, ti, do, fa, la, sol, mi, ti, re."

Seryozha stood up. Olga stood up too. They helped Rebrov to put the cube down onto the floor. Rebrov took his arms out of the straps, picked up the chisel, and began to pry open the nailed-down lid.

"Opa!" Shtaube climbed out of the cube and hopped on one leg over to his prosthesis. Olga helped him to put it on and picked his long, green breeches up from the floor.

"I can do that myself, Olga Vladimirovna. Thank you," he took the breeches from her, leaned against the wall, and nimbly put them on.

"Everything was perfect," Rebrov removed the nails from the plywood and put the lid back on. "Everything was completely, totally adequate, just speak more distinctly, Seryozha, and don't swallow the ends of your words."

"Mhmm," Seryozha was sitting on the floor and pulling up his socks.

"And sharpness, sharpness," Shtaube remarked. "Speak sharply and clearly. Ta! Ta! Ta!"

When everyone was dressed, Rebrov looked at his watch.

"Okay. Let's move."

They went into the hallway and began to put on their outer layers.

"The canisters, Henry Ivanych," said Rebrov.

Shtaube took three canisters out of his pocket.

"One for you and one for both Olga Vladimirovna and me," Rebrov took a canister and Olga took the other.

"And the rags?" Seryozha asked, putting on his hat.

"Yes! The rags!" Rebrov remembered. "In the bathroom."

He walked into the bathroom and came back with four wet, woolen rags.

"Here. One for everyone. Please pay attention. You'll hold it in your left hand, so keep it in your left pocket in the meantime. And now . . . the support?"

Olga patted the inner pocket of her jacket.

"Right here."

Shtaube reached his hand into his jacket pocket.

"Yes, yes."

"Fantastic," Rebrov put on his leather hat. "And the key?"

Seryozha handed him a key chain.

"Is that everything?" Rebrov locked eyes with Olga.

She nodded.

"Well, let's move," he opened the door.

"God be with us," Shtaube whispered, then left the apartment, and began to walk down the stairs. The others followed him down.

In the courtyard, Rebrov and Olga headed for a grey Zhiguli, while the old man and young boy walked through an arch and out onto the street. Rebrov started the car, turned, and pulled out onto the street. Shtaube and Seryozha got in next to a ruined newsstand.

"How long have they been searching for you, Seryozha?" Rebrov asked, beginning to drive along the Garden Ring.

"Three months and six days," the boy replied.

"Three months!" Shtaube shook his head. "How time flies . . ."

"That means all the dogs around your building will still recognize you," said Rebrov.

"They will," Seryozha nodded, "the old ladies sitting on the benches too."

"Is there a bench near your entrance?"

"It's fine, I'll get him past," Olga struck a match and lit up.

"Would it be better to go at night?" proposed Shtaube.

"Madness. The whole building would be asleep and everyone'd hear . . ."

"I'll get him past, no one'll recognize him!"

"Okay then."

They passed by Zubovsky Square and turned onto Frunzenskaya Embankment just before the Crimean Bridge.

"So, here's how we'll do it," began Rebrov. "First, I'll walk in, then Henry Ivanych. And then you and Seryozha."

"Whatever you say," sighed Shtaube.

"Now, Seryozha, tell me . . ."

"Just a sec, here's 'Gastronom' and the next one's ours. Mine."

"Okay. Then let's stop right here."

Rebrov turned and parked the car right up against the curb behind a beige Volga.

"Again," he turned to them, "Remember the rags. And the support, just in case. I'm counting on you for that, Olga Vladimirovna."

"Don't worry," Olga smiled.

"The third entrance. Turn right there," indicated Seryozha.

Rebrov got out of the car and walked into the building's courtyard. Two old women were sitting on a bench next to the third entrance. He flipped up the collar of his coat and walked briskly into the building. He climbed the stairs to the third floor and stopped next to the garbage chute.

Four minutes later, Shtaube came up in the elevator. Olga and Seryozha appeared almost immediately after him.

"There," Rebrov showed the way with a jerk of his head and they walked over to a soundly upholstered door. He took out a key, but immediately put it back into his pocket. "No. Ring the bell."

"Twice?"

"Yes. Olya."

Olga unbuttoned her jacket. Seryozha rang.

"Who's there?" a woman's voice asked from behind the door.

"It's me, Mommy," Seryozha replied.

The door opened and Seryozha immediately threw his arms around the neck of the petite blonde standing in the threshold.

"Mommy! Mom!"

"Sergei! Sergei! Sergei!" the woman cried out, squeezing Seryozha. "Kolya! Kolya! Sergei!"

A thin man ran over to them, grabbed on to Seryozha's head, and squeezed it.

"Sergei! Sergei! Sergei!" the woman cried out.

"Mommy, Daddy, hold on . . . I'm not alone . . ."

"Sergei! Sergei! I can't! I can't!" the woman was trembling.

The man was weeping silently.

"Mommy . . . I'm here, I'm alive, Mommy, hold on."

"Don't worry, Lydia Petrovna, the worst is behind you," proclaimed Rebrov, smiling.

"Yes. Thank God," Shtaube smirked.

"I can't! Sergei!" the woman was shivering and clutching on to Seryozha.

"Mommy . . . hold on, this . . . this is Viktor Valentinovich and this is Olga Vladimirovna, they're from the criminal investigations department . . . Mommy . . ."

The man was the first to come to his senses.

"Come in, come in . . . Please . . ." he wiped his face with his palms and pulled the woman by the arm. "Calm down, Lida, everything's fine, just fine."

"Mom . . . come on, Mommy, hold on . . ."

"Yes, yes, come in . . . Seryozha, oy, Seryozha," when she was done embracing Seryozha, she took him off to the side.

Rebrov, Olga, and Shtaube entered. The man shut the door behind them.

"Just yesterday I called your . . . well, I called Fedchenko," the man began to speak with some difficulty. "And he just says . . . this . . . we're looking, we're looking."

"You called yesterday. Not today," Rebrov smiled.

"Oy, my heart's gonna burst!" the woman put her hands to her temples and began to shake her head. "Sergei, Sergei . . . what have you done to us?"

"He's not the only one responsible," Rebrov spoke up.

"Everyone turned out to be responsible," Olga added quietly.

"Oy . . . well, come in, don't just stand there," the woman walked into the room, not letting go of Seryozha.

"Just for a minute," Rebrov said and everyone walked into the room.

"Where were you? Where could you've been?" the woman shook her head.

"Yes, you've really done a number on . . ." the man sat down on the couch, but, having remembered something, jumped back up. "Sit down, comrades, what are you . . ."

"Thank you, but we don't have time to sit," Rebrov put his hands into the pockets of his jacket. "Tell them, Seryozha. About our surprise."

"Yes, Mom, we have a surprise," Seryozha broke out of his mother's embrace. "Here, Mom and Dad, sit on the couch and listen. Just don't interrupt."

"Not interrupting might be difficult," Olga grinned.

"We'll try not to," the woman sat down on the couch with a sigh. The man sat next to her.

"Now the rags," Rebrov pronounced calmly.

All four of them pulled out the wet rags and put them to their faces, covering their noses and mouths. Rebrov brandished the gas canister in his right hand and sprayed it into the faces of the man and the woman. Screaming helplessly, they grabbed at their mouths and slid down from the couch and onto the floor.

"Get back, move away!" Rebrov commanded, running away from the fallen parents, and everyone backed over to the window.

A shudder passed over the bodies of the man and woman and they froze in unnatural positions.

Without removing the rag from his face, Rebrov put the gas canister back into his pocket.

"Olya. Do it calmly."

Pressing the rag to her face with her left hand, Olga took a sport pistol with a folding handle and a cylindrical silencer on the end of its barrel from the inside of her jacket and walked over to the man and the woman sprawled out on the floor.

"It doesn't need to be point-blank," Shtaube interjected.

Having taken quick and skillful aim, Olga shot the man and the woman in the head.

"And another," Rebrov commanded.

Two more muffled claps rang out, the heads of the man and the woman jerked, and empty bullet casings rolled across the floor.

"And another thirty seconds." Rebrov waited for a little while, then put the rag into his pocket. "It's alright."

Everyone put away their rags. Olga put the gun back into the interior pocket of her jacket and Seryozha picked up the four bullet casings.

Rebrov threw open the left side of his coat and, from separate pockets, pulled out a large pair of surgical scissors, a test tube with a stopper, and a vial of clear liquid.

"First the mother," Rebrov handed the test tube and the vial to Shtaube. Olga and Seryozha turned the woman's corpse onto its back. Her face was covered in blood and her eye had come out of its socket.

"Henry Ivanych," mumbled Rebrov, kneeling down to the face of the corpse with the scissors.

Shtaube uncorked the test tube and handed it over. Rebrov cut the woman's lips off quickly and put them into the test tube. Shtaube poured the clear fluid from the vial over the lips and put the stopper back in.

"So," Rebrov wiped his bloody hand on the corpse's cardigan, "now the father."

Olga and Seryozha turned the man's corpse over, unbuttoned his pants, pulled them down, then pulled down his underwear.

"Seryozha!" Rebrov pulled out the penis, pulled back its foreskin, cut off the glans, and quickly put it into Seryozha's mouth as the boy knelt down. Seryozha began to suck the glans, gently rolling it around in his mouth. Olga wiped his lips with a handkerchief.

"Is the jewelry box in the bedroom?" Rebrov took a handkerchief from Olga and wiped off the scissors.

Seryozha nodded and waved his hand. Olga left. Rebrov put the test tube with the lips, the vial, and the scissors into his coat. Olga came back holding a small oriental jewelry box. Rebrov took a black nylon bag out of his pocket and Olga put the jewelry box into it.

"So," Rebrov looked around. "Is that everything?"

"The only thing is I'd like to drink a lil' water," Shtaube limped into the kitchen.

"You don't want to take anything with you?" Rebrov asked Seryozha.

Seryozha was sucking the glans with great concentration.

"Seryozha?" Olga touched the boy on the shoulder.

He looked at her and shook his head. But then he suddenly left the room, returning almost immediately with a plush crocodile. The crocodile was old and torn in several places.

"A-a-ah. Well, well," Rebrov nodded and glanced at the corpses. "Alright, let's move."

They walked out of the room and into the hallway.

Her face was covered in blood and her eye had come out of its socket.

"Are you coming, Henry Ivanych?" Rebrov walked over to the door.

"I'm coming, I'm coming." Shtaube came out of the kitchen.

"So, you and I will be first, followed by Olga and Seryozha."

"Gotcha."

Rebrov opened the door and left. Shtaube followed him out.

Olga shut the door behind them and leaned against it. Seryozha looked the crocodile over and sucked on the glans.

"Did you miss him?" asked Olga.

He nodded.

"Have you had him for a long time?"

Seryozha held up three fingers.

"Three years? Then how did he get so beat up?"

"It . . . was . . . Gr-grandma's," he said with difficulty.

Olga pressed her ear to the door and listened. Seryozha also pressed himself to the door.

"Okay. Let's go." Olga opened the door.

They left, Olga carefully shut the door, took Seryozha by the hand, and led him down the stairs.

"Same behavior downstairs," she muttered.

As they were walking out, Seryozha grabbed Olga with both hands and began to growl.

"Stop it, Vitya!" she said loudly.

Seryozha pressed his face to her jacket and began to growl even more loudly.

"Vitya, Vitya!" she laughed. "You're a big boy, stop it!"

They walked through the door and passed by some old women sitting on the bench. A heavy snow was falling.

Embracing, they walked through the courtyard and turned toward the car. Seeing them, Rebrov started the engine and began to turn.

"So, you didn't choke on it?" Olga opened the back door of the Zhiguli.

"Uh-uh," Seryozha replied, climbing into the car with the crocodile.

Olga looked around unhurriedly, then sat next to him.

"A success?" Rebrov accelerated.

"A success," Olga rested her head against the seat, filled with relief.

"Did you turn off the light?"

"No."

"That's a shame," Rebrov turned onto the embankment.

"You didn't say to," Olga took out her cigarette case and opened it.

"Olga Vladimirovna," growled Shtaube, "you're not a child."

"I'm not a child," Olga blew on a cigarette, then lit up.

"Give me one too," Rebrov held out his hand and Olga lay a cigarette into it.

Rebrov began to smoke, exhaling forcefully.

"That's terrible. But . . . fair enough, what can we do."

"I can go back," Olga smirked.

"Oh, that's an idea!" snorted Shtaube. "Go back. Good that comes too late is as good as nothing, Olga Vladimirovna."

"When did your uncle promise to come, Seryozha?" asked Rebrov.

The boy spat his father's glans into his hand.

"On New Year's."

Rebrov nodded. Turned onto the Garden Ring.

Olga pulled out the pistol, removed the clip, and put four new bullets into it. Seryozha examined the glans.

"If you're going to suck it, then really suck it." Olga pulled back the slide.

The boy put the glans into his mouth and began to twirl the crocodile around.

"I was at the Cheremushkinsky Market today," said Rebrov.

"Was it expensive?" Shtaube asked.

"Meat was between fifteen and twenty-five. Pickles were seven. Pears were ten."

"Gosh," Shtaube shook his head. "What a rip-off!"

"Did you buy any rosehip oil?" Olga put away the gun.

"Yes."

"How was your trip to Petersburg, Olga Vladimirovna?" Shtaube asked.

"Terrible."

"Really? Did something happen?"

"Yes, it's a sad story," Rebrov grimaced as smoke drifted into his eyes. "A story of human squalor, callousness, and indifference."

"I arrived in the morning, visited Boris, and brought him the cicatricials. Then went to see Ilya Anatolich and gave him the cobbler's wax and a fourth. He lives outside of the city and it took so long to get back, just so long. I was damn tired. So I went to see my grandma, like always. I'm thinking I'll get to take a bath and drink some cognac . . ."

"Oh yeah, you love that!" Shtaube laughed.

"I arrive and ring the doorbell. Nothing. I ring for a whole hour. Then I check in with the neighbors. They've been living there for fifteen years and they don't even know her name. They say they haven't seen her for a while. I call Maria Markovna, her only friend. She hasn't gotten through to Grandma for a month. 'I call, I call, and no one answers,' she says. She's also eighty-two, but she doesn't really get out much. Grandma did everything by herself, even went to the store alone, absolutely everything. So. I go to the building's super. We get a policeman, a locksmith, and some witnesses. We break down the door. Then the smell hits us and we realize. We go in. And . . ."

"That's enough, Olga Vladimirovna, I'm begging you," Shtaube put his hands over his ears.

"So I . . . for the first time in my life, I saw a person filled with worms. My wormy grandma. All that was left was skin filled with worms. From the way they were moving, it almost seemed like Grandma was trying to crawl. People came from the morgue and needed an oilcloth to lift her body. And when they took her away . . ."

"Olga Vladimirovna! Olga Vladimirovna! I'm begging you! I'm really begging you!" cried Shtaube, squeezing his ears shut. "If I'm begging, if I'm really begging! Then why do you! Then!"

"Forgive me, Shtaube, my darling. I'm just very tired," Olga leaned back against the seat. "I've come straight here from the wake."

"It's horrible, horrible," Shtaube shook his head. "Nobody comes and nobody calls. What kind of people have we become! My God!"

"Yes," Rebrov sighed. "We marvel at the callousness of the youth. And yet we are all guilty."

"No, I can still remember the war and just after the war!" Shtaube took off his hat and smoothed his grey hair. "How hard it was, how badly we lived! But I don't remember people being indifferent! People were boorish, stingy, and savage, but never indifferent! Never, never indifferent!"

Seryozha spat the glans into his palm.

"Am I not indifferent?"

"You're alright," Rebrov smiled.

"You're our little Timur," Olga laughed. "Timur separated from his detachment. What is it? Are you tired of sucking? Give it to me then . . ."

Bending over, she picked up the glans from Seryozha's hand with her lips and shook her head.

"Is it good?" asked Seryozha.

Olga nodded.

They turned onto Mir Prospect. Heavy flakes of snow were falling. They passed onto Yaroslavl Highway, turned right. The highway entered into a snowy forest and, three kilometers later, they stopped at the gates of a green, three-meter-high fence.

Rebrov honked.

"Oo-f-f . . . are we there already?" Shtaube groaned, putting on his hat.

"Why is there more snow here than in Moscow, Viktor Valentinych?" Seryozha asked.

"We went north. It's colder."

A door opened next to the gates and a policeman with a sheepskin coat thrown over his shoulders walked out.

They turned onto Mir Prospect. Heavy flakes of snow were falling.

Rebrov rolled down the window.

"Good evening! Are you snowed under yet?"

"Welcome," the policeman walked over, looked inside, turned around, and walked back through the door.

The gates opened slowly. The car began to drive through.

"Would you happen to have a cigarette?" the policeman stood up against the small guardhouse.

"We *would* happen to," Rebrov braked. "Where're our cigarettes, Ninochka?"

Olga handed him the cigarette case. Rebrov opened it and held it out to the policeman.

"Thank you. Is Igor Ivanovich not coming?"

"No. Probably not before the new year."

The policeman struck a match. They drove further along the narrow, snow-covered highway. In the thick, coniferous forest, they could occasionally glimpse the outlines of dachas. They turned right and drove up to another gate. Rebrov got out, unlocked it, and opened it.

"Shut it behind me, Seryozha."

The car drove through the gate. Seryozha jumped out, shut the gate, and scurried back in. A hundred meters later, a large, two-story house appeared among the pines. They drove up to it and stopped. They began to get out.

"Oy," Shtaube frowned as he limped toward the house. "We need to clear a path, Viktor Valentinych . . ."

Rebrov took two bags from the trunk.

"Tomorrow, we'll do everything tomorrow."

Seryozha made a snowball and threw it at Olga's back. Without turning around, Olga shook her fist at him.

They entered the house. Shtaube turned on a light. They got undressed in the entrance hallway and hung their clothes on enormous moose antlers. Rebrov handed Olga a brown bag.

"Take that to the kitchen right away. And cook it."

"Yes, Olga Vladimirovna, cook, cook, I'm begging you to cook," Shtaube carefully removed his galoshes. "I had lunch at twelve at a hideous diner. I'm terribly hungry."

"And I didn't eat lunch at all." Seryozha deftly threw his hat onto the antlers. "Can I go look at Vorontsov, Viktor Valentinych?"

"Hold on, we'll all go."

"But can't I just go?!"

"No, no. I need you now. Let's go to the office." Carrying a black bag, Rebrov began to climb the wide, carpeted stairs to the second floor.

"Well . . ." hitting his own leg with the crocodile, the boy followed him reluctantly.

Olga rattled through the dishes in the kitchen. Shtaube disappeared into the bathroom.

Rebrov entered the office, turned on a desk lamp, took the jewelry box out of the bag, and put it on the table. Took out the test tube with the lips and examined them in the light.

"So."

Seryozha was looking over the spines of the many books.

"What are thermodynamics, Viktor Valentinych?"

"Thermodynamics?" Rebrov put the test tube into a case next to other test tubes. "Honestly, I don't really know . . . come over here please."

Rebrov opened the box. Seryozha walked over. The box was filled with papers, money, a bundle of letters, pieces of jewelry in plush boxes, and a pair of theater binoculars edged in mother of pearl.

"Nikolai Nikolaevich Anishchenko," Rebrov opened a passport and read from it. "Repeat what you just said about the mustache."

"He had a mustache when we moved from Mokhovaya, then he grew a beard twice and didn't have a mustache. And the last time, for the last year, I mean, he only had a mustache."

"So." Rebrov opened a notebook, began to take notes in it, then took out a pair of scissors, and began to cut the pictures out of the passport. "Say what you said about chess."

"Well," Seryozha put the crocodile on the edge of the table and bent its tail, "every Sunday, at the Park of Culture, in the chess pavilion. You would see Sergei Ivanych, and Kolya, and some Tolik."

"The guy with the bad joint?"

"Mhmm."

Rebrov put the pictures into an envelope.

"Can I take the binoculars?" asked Seryozha.

Rebrov shook his head.

"That won't be possible . . . That's enough for today. Tomorrow we'll talk about the fat man and about the ribs. Now, go watch cartoons."

The boy lifted the crocodile over his head and left.

Olga cooked veal with stewed quince and fried potatoes for dinner. They drank a bottle of champagne. Rebrov ate and drank in silence. Shtaube told them about postal pigeons and his voyage down the Volga on a vessel called the *Maxim Gorky*. After having ice cream with nuts and tea, Rebrov lit a cigarette, running his hand exhaustedly across his forehead.

"Well . . . thank you, Olga Vladimirovna. Shall we go see Vorontsov?"

"Yes! Yes!" Shtaube exclaimed, wiping his lips with a napkin. "Let's go before it's too late, which would be . . . bad."

"Henry Ivanovich," Olga pointed to the glans floating in a glass of water.

"Yes, yes," Shtaube picked up the glans and laid it carefully into his mouth. Everyone stood up from the table.

"Go. I'll follow," Olga lit a cigarette and went into the kitchen. Rebrov, Shtaube, and Seryozha walked into a dark room next to the kitchen. The room's four walls were covered in shelves tightly packed with canned food, alcohol, and other provisions. In the middle of the floor was a cellar door fastened shut with a latch. Rebrov undid the latch and opened the door. The smell of human feces wafted up from the dark hatch. The hatch was covered with a metal grille. Rebrov took an electric flashlight from the wall and shined it down into the hatch.

"Good evening, Andrei Borisovich."

A man began to move around at the bottom of a deep concrete dungeon. He had no legs, no right hand, and was lying in his own excrement, which had formed a thick layer on the floor of the bunker. He was wearing a quilted jacket and an assortment of rags, all of which were covered in feces. There was a dynamo generator attached to an electric heater in the corner.

"And I . . ." Vorontsov said in a hoarse voice, looking up.

His bearded face was thin and brown with feces.

"How are things?" Rebrov shined the light onto Vorontsov. "Is the generator working? You're not cold?"

"Well . . . all of it . . . works and works properly," Vorontsov spoke up, was quiet, then began to speak quickly and unintelligibly: "Georgii Adamovich, I, I, I'm chafing constantly and ready to twist, well, there, when it becomes necessary, everything will and already does work, I know about all the, well, opportunities, so to speak, and I learned from the last incident and am ready to be corrected, ready for, well, various things, ready to be in shape and know what I need and what you need to know, I'm ready to know that which it is necessary to know."

"Fantastic," Rebrov nodded. "Your stump isn't bleeding?"

"And I . . . I . . . this . . ." Vorontsov shook his head. "That here I am . . . here . . . like all that which is necessary."

He quickly took the stump of his hand, bound in rags, out of the pocket of his jacket and showed it to them.

Rebrov nodded and looked over at Shtaube. Shtaube gave him the thumbs up.

Olga came in with a large bowl of boiled potatoes, on top of which was a piece of bread and a piece of lard. Olga put the bowl onto the grate and knocked her cigarette ash into the bunker.

"Hi, Vorontsov."

Vorontsov began to move, crawling over to the opposite wall and looking continuously upward.

"Ah . . . Tatyana Isaakova . . . I . . . just . . ."

"Does he not have any poppy seeds again?" Olga asked. Rebrov nodded. Seryozha took a potato and dropped it down the hatch. Vorontsov fell to the ground, covered the potato with his left hand, pulled it over, and began to smack his lips.

"So," Rebrov clapped his hands together. "Let's begin, Andrei Borisovich, you disappointed us last time. Disappointed us so much that, I'll admit it, I was ready to throw in the towel. And let me assure you that I would have done so if I weren't such a kind and good-hearted person by nature. That's the first reason. The second reason is that Boris Ivanovich," he looked over at Shtaube, "interceded on your behalf."

Shtaube nodded.

"So today is your last chance, Andrei Borisovich. Take it seriously. Understand that your future lies in your hands."

"In your head," Olga added.

"Yes, yes," Rebrov nodded, then raised his voice louder than normal and asked, "so, Vorontsov, are you ready?"

Vorontsov crawled to the center of the bunker and sat up.

"I yes. I yes."

"In that case, No. 1 please."

Vorontsov cleared his throat and began to speak, diligently enunciating each word.

"If I am fond of the sea and of all that is of the sea's kind, and fondest when it angrily contradicts me; if that delight in searching which drives the sails toward the undiscovered is in me, if a seafarer's delight is in my delight; if ever my jubilation cried, 'The coast has vanished, now the last chain has fallen from me; the boundless roars around me, far out glisten space and time; be of good cheer, old heart!' Oh, how should I not lust after eternity and after the nuptial ring of rings, the ring of recurrence? Never yet have I found the woman from whom I wanted children, unless it be this woman whom I love: for I love you, O Eternity."[1]

He stopped, looking continuously upward.

"No. 2," Rebrov demanded after a short pause.

"I this, this yes . . . here. The act of defecation is complex reflex action, in which the cerebral cortex, the pathways of the spinal cord, the peripheral nerves of the rectum, the abdominal muscles, and the large intestine all participate. The reflex to defecate arises in the rectum when it is irritated by a mass of feces and, consequently, it is not only a route for immediate evacuation, but also a place for the temporary accumulation of fecal mass. There are several different types of defecation: one-moment defecation and two- or sometimes even many-moment defecation. During the first type of defecation, everything happens quickly, in a moment: after several compressions of the abdominal muscles, all of the content accumulated in the rectum and the sigmoid colon is expelled . . ."

"And what is the sigmoid colon?" Olga asked loudly.

"The sigmoid colon . . . the sigmoid colon is a section of the large intestine located above the rectum, which itself is the continuation of the lower part of the large intestine. During the second type of defecation, two-moment defecation, during the first moment, only some of the fecal content accumulated in the rectum is expelled. A few minutes later, after the first portion of fecal matter has been expelled, a peristaltic contraction pushes the contents of the sigmoid colon into the rectum, resulting in a second urge to defecate."

Rebrov sighed and looked at Olga. She rubbed her temples wearily and yawned. Shtaube sucked the glans angrily. Seryozha mouthed the inscriptions on the labels of foreign bottles.

"No. 3," pronounced Rebrov.

"Examples of skulls that have been intentionally opened at their

---

1. From the Walter Kaufmann translation of Nietzsche's *Thus Spake Zarathustra*.

base apparently in order to get to the brain," Vorontsov, visibly relieved, began to speak quickly, "are regarded as evidence of cannibalism. Up on the left, Steinheim's skull, up on the right, the skull of a Neanderthal from Monte Circeo, lower down is a modern Papuan skull from New Guinea and a prehistoric find from Moravia. An accumulation of Mesolithic skulls. A tomb uncovered in the Grotte du Cavillon near Grimaldi, Italy. Three large stone tools of archaic design made of solid volcanic rock. Northern Australia. A unique little harpoon with three rows of smooth . . ."

"That's enough, enough, enough, for the love of God! I can't take it!" Angered, Shtaube suddenly screamed and spat the glans into his hand.

Vorontsov fell silent.

"Viktor Valentinovich!" said Shtaube indignantly. "If you deign to mock yourself, to mock your own soul, then at least spare our souls!"

"And our ears," Olga added quietly and sighed heavily. "Horrible, how horrible everything is . . ."

"Now what . . . the ghoul?" Seryozha turned to them.

"One must not indulge scoundrels! One must not! I'm an old man, Viktor Valentinovich, and can understand and forgive many human weaknesses, I'm a Christian! I can forgive ignorance, rudeness, cruelty, even beastliness! But not mockery of the human soul! Never! And you . . ." he bent down toward the grate, "you are . . . a scoundrel! If you . . . spit on, if you neglect, if you . . ." Shtaube's voice trembled. "If you . . . you . . . know that . . . no! My God . . ."

He turned around and left the pantry.

Olga extinguished the butt of her cigarette on the edge of a shelf, dropped it into the hatch, and followed Shtaube out.

"So, the ghoul again" Seryozha walked over to Shtaube.

"Seryozha," Rebrov took the bowl of potatoes off of the grille. "Take this to the kitchen, please."

"Sir yes sir," Seryozha picked up the bowl and left.

Rebrov was silent for a long time, folding his arms across his chest and lowering his head. Then he began to speak.

"Mhmm. Well, Andrei Borisovich, let's sum things up. You have reached no conclusions over the last four days, that's one. I overestimated your moral foundation, that's two. I underestimated your plebeian pragmatism. Three. To sentence you to a fourth amputation would be banal, and, in this case, devoid of any sense. Our decision was known to you in advance."

Rebrov slammed the cellar door down with a bang and latched it shut. He picked up the flashlight, put it up onto a shelf, and left.

Shtaube, Olga, and Seryozha were waiting for him in the dining room. Olga was clearing dirty dishes, the old man was sucking the glans angrily, and Seryozha was twisting a Rubik's cube.

Rebrov walked over to the table, absentmindedly grabbed an apple from a bowl, and took a bite.

"Henry Ivanych and I both warned you," Olga said.

Rebrov walked over to the window. Outside the window it was dark and snow was falling.

"Didn't he count with his fingers, Ol? Didn't he do anything?" Seryozha asked.

Olga shook her head.

"He's nothing more than a hongweibing!" Shtaube spat the glans into his hand. "I told you more than a month ago, Viktor Valentinovich, when you did the first test! This guy is completely amoral! He's a thinking animal! This scoundrel took advantage of your mercifulness with his incredible cold-bloodedness and his really quite infernal impudence!"

"Took advantage of *our* mercifulness," interjected Olga.

"And then, what kind of tone is that? What kind of tropino is that? Why, for example, was he silent before the holiday and why did he show us just three fingers? And why is it all down the drain now? Why are there no phails? And why have we ended up acting the fool again?"

Rebrov chewed his apple, looking out the window.

"And you know," Seryozha looked at the cube he'd solved, "Henry Ivanych tried to *rob cradles* again today."

Rebrov turned around. Olga froze, a plate in her hands. Shtaube began to get up from his chair, clutching the glans in his fist.

"Henry Ivanych," pronounced Rebrov and, dropping the apple, threw himself onto Shtaube.

"No! You fucking!" Shtaube cried, swinging his cane at Seryozha, but Rebrov grabbed his arm and twisted it behind his back.

Olga grabbed the old man's left hand.

"The glans! Give us the glans!"

"You fucking! Fucking! Little shit!" Shtaube cried.

Rebrov squeezed the old man's throat and he wheezed and fell to his knees. Rebrov threw his cane off to the side. Olga tore open the old man's fingers and immediately threw the glans into Seryozha's open mouth.

"Get the bandage and the handcuffs, Seryozha!" Rebrov commanded.

Seryozha ran off.

"You . . . you just shit . . . I won't allow . . ." Shtaube wheezed in Rebrov's arms.

"You signed the document! You signed! How could you! Olga, get the sofa, the sofa . . ."

Olga moved a narrow leather sofa away from the wall.

Seryozha ran in with a bandage and handcuffs.

"No . . . bas . . . tards . . . you yourselves are . . . no . . ." Shtaube wheezed.

Rebrov and Olga dragged him over to the sofa and put him onto it facedown.

"Seryozha," Rebrov commanded.

Seryozha bound the old man's mouth with the bandage. Then, the three of them worked to wrap the old man's hands around a leg of the sofa and to put the handcuffs on them. Rebrov sat on Shtaube's leg, while Seryozha grabbed tightly on to his prosthesis.

"Olga Vladimirovna, in my office, in the desk, in the bottom drawer, on the left. Put it on the big hotplate. It'll heat up faster."

"I know," Olga left quickly.

"Where did it happen?" asked Rebrov.

"Right . . . on Novatorov. Just after Borisovo. I ran out for chewing gum, then came back. And Henry Ivanych was at the bakery . . ."

Rebrov nodded grimly. Shtaube was breathing plaintively through his nose.

"Henry Ivanych," Rebrov said slowly, "you've really upset me today. Really upset me. To stab us in the back like that . . . it's very painful, you know. It's beastly."

He stood up and began to unbutton the old man's pants. Shtaube whined. Seryozha helped Rebrov. They pulled the old man's worn, black trousers down to his knees and pulled down his underpants. Rebrov rolled the old man's shirt and sweater up his back. There were two brands in the shape of an encircled cross, each the size of a ruble, on Shtaube's left buttock. One brand was very old, the other, judging by its dark-purple color, was more recent.

"Our union, Henry Ivanovich, our friendship does not rest only on mutual love. But also on very concrete mutual obligations. In insulting and humiliating yourself, you also insult and humiliate us. Piss in the cup, Seryozha."

The boy let go of the prosthesis, walked over to the table, and urinated a little bit into a cup.

Olga came in holding a small satchel and a thick steel rod with a wooden handle, at the end of which was a steel brand: an encircled cross. The brand had already been heated up.

Shtaube thrashed and groaned. Rebrov pushed his leg harder against the sofa.

"Next to Borodinsky, here . . . Seryozha! The prosthesis . . ."

Seryozha put the cup of urine on the floor and grabbed on to the prosthesis. Olga aimed, then pressed the brand to the old man's buttock. The hot steel hissed, producing a tiny puff of steam, and Shtaube thrashed against the sofa. Olga removed the brand, picked up the cup, and poured urine onto the crimson brand. Then she opened the bag, took out a vial of rosehip oil and a cotton ball and began to carefully swab the burn.

"There . . . my sweet Shtaube . . . it's all over . . ."

The old man's head was trembling and tears were pouring from his eyes.

"Now the carotid, Olga Vladimirovna, the carotid right now," Rebrov muttered.

Olga unhurriedly sealed the vial, took out and unwrapped a disposable syringe, and attached a needle to it.

"Hold his head down, Seryozha . . ."

The boy pressed Shtaube's head to the sofa. Olga gave an ampoule a flick, broke it open, and pulled all of its contents into the syringe. Shtaube wept and whined.

"Now my dear . . ." she skillfully stuck the needle into his carotid artery, slowly injecting him with a clear liquid. Shtaube's whole body jerked, he moaned slowly, and he coughed through his nose. Seryozha let go of his head and it came to rest on its side. Rebrov got off of the old man's legs and carefully took the bandage from the old man's mouth.

"Until . . . through the loops . . ." the old man said in a weak voice. "You . . . you're not . . . bad . . ."

Rebrov took his handcuffs off. Olga covered the burn with oil-soaked gauze and put the bandage on it. Shtaube slept. They undressed him completely, removed his prosthesis, and took him into the bedroom, where they put his pajamas on and put him to bed.

"Let him sleep as late as he wants tomorrow." Rebrov covered Shtaube with a thick, quilted blanket.

"Of course, no one's gonna wake him up," Olga stroked the old man's head.

Seryozha spat the glans into his hand.

"Well, I'm gonna watch a movie."

"A movie, Seryozha?" Rebrov looked at his watch. "It's already past midnight. Go to bed immediately. We have a lot of things to do tomorrow."

The boy gave him the glans with a sigh.

"G'night."

"Good night."

"Good night, Seryozhenka," Olga kissed him. The boy left.

"I'm exhausted . . ." Rebrov rubbed his temples.

"Do you want some cognac?" Olga asked.

He nodded distractedly.

"Let's sit by the fireplace."

"By the fireplace?" Rebrov looked at the glans, then at Shtaube sleeping. "Let's move."

Olga turned off the light and Rebrov put the glans into his mouth.

Rebrov sat in an armchair and stared into the roaring fireplace. Sitting cross-legged on the rug, Olga poured a second portion of cognac into their glasses.

"Where once the cheerful scythe felled ears of grain, now emptiness reigns . . . empty space everywhere . . ." Rebrov muttered and sighed wearily. "Yes, yes, yes. If we don't manage to reach Kovshov on Thursday, I'm done with this shit. I'll go to Kiev."

"What about us?" Olga handed him his glass.

"You? You . . ." he sipped the cognac. "I really, really don't know. You'll go on your own, you'll get there on your own."

"What are you saying," Olga smiled. "How will we get there on our own?"

He jerked his head in frustration.

"Olga Vladimirovna! I've been banging my head against this wall for three whole months. I've lost: Golubovsky, Lydia Moiseyevna, and the Tsvetkovs. We lost a whole block. Henry Ivanych burned down the greenhouses. You abandoned the third part of the equipment. Sergei doesn't remember anything about Denis and I don't think he *will* remember anything about him. That means we'll be forced to get crub and to get Berentsovians through Leningrad. And only through Leningrad. That's an inventory of our losses. And what have we gained? A ruined workshop decayed to its very core? Connections that don't matter to anyone? Naiman's pointless calculations? Six million other useless things?"

"But Kovshov promised . . ."

"Kovshov? Promised? Have you ever even seen him with your own eyes? No. I haven't seen him either. In our position, trusting someone at the other end of a telephone line is obviously idiotic. But a necessary idiocy. That's why I accepted this arrangement. No, no, we have nothing but palliatives. A thick swath of dependencies and forced hands."

"But Vitya, we're done with the metal. Naiman said his guys succeeded."

"His guys succeeded! Yes! But that doesn't necessarily imply that we'll succeed. If you're so certain, why did you vote against it? On principle? Or was it actually because you weren't sure?"

Olga drank silently from her glass. Rebrov gulped down his cognac and put the glass on the floor.

"Of course, optimism is good. It's what stops us from giving up. While we work, we do what we can. But we must also rely on probability and hard calculations. And throw away all of our rainbow-tinted fantasies. Once and for all."

He went quiet, looked into the fire, then said, "Olga Vladimirovna. Let's fuck."

Olga raised her eyebrows in surprise.

"What . . . right now?"

He nodded. Olga glanced at the outline of his erect penis in his pants out of the corner of her eye, smiled, and began to undress. Rebrov stood up and took off his pants and underwear. When they were both undressed, Olga walked over to Rebrov. He turned her around and she

He went quiet, looked into the fire, then said, "Olga Vladimirovna. Let's fuck."

rested her elbows on the back of a leather chair. Rebrov entered her from behind and began to thrust impatiently, moaning loudly. Olga pressed her cheek against the back of the chair and stared into the fire. Rebrov began to thrust faster, leaned back, then grabbed Olga by the shoulders, pressed himself against her, froze, and growled into her hair.

"Vitya . . ." she whispered and smiled.

"Oy . . . I even started to drool . . ." Rebrov wiped his mouth with his hand, walked away, and collapsed exhaustedly onto the sofa. "Oy . . . Olga Vladimirovna . . . forgive me . . . please . . ."

"For what?" she rubbed her hand between her legs, then sniffed it.

"Forgive me . . . forgive me for everything," he mumbled.

"I'll be right back," she left and came back five minutes later, tying the belt of a white terry dressing gown.

Rebrov was asleep on the sofa. Olga brought him a blanket, covered him with it, picked up his clothes, put the glans into a glass, and went to her room.

Seryozha woke up before everyone else. The sun was shining outside the window. The clock showed 9:22. Seryozha slid out from underneath his blanket, stretched, and stood up. He was wearing red underwear and a white T-shirt with the logo of the rock band the Rolling Stones. He went into the hall, walked up to Olga's door, and cautiously began to open it. The room was dark because of the tightly shut purple curtains. Olga was sleeping. Seryozha walked in quietly, shut the door behind him, walked over to the bed, and began to slowly pull the blanket off of Olga.

"Once upon a time while touring the district, Father Onufrii came upon a naked Olga . . ."

Olga exhaled.

"Seryozhenka . . ."

"Give yourself to me, Olga, I'll shower you with gold," Seryozha touched her bosom.

She yawned, turned onto her back, and opened her eyes.

"What time is it?"

"Twenty-five fucks after nine," Seryozha's hand slid down to her groin.

Olga slapped his hand away and sat up.

"Open the . . . curtains . . ."

Seryozha pulled the cord, the curtains opened, and sunlight flooded the room.

"Oy, how lovely," Olga blinked and rubbed her eyes. "Let's go skiing . . . is Viktor up?"

"I'm not gonna tell."

She reached for her dressing gown, but Seryozha grabbed it and sat up on the windowsill.

"Chick, chick, chick."

"Asshole . . . ooouuuuaa!" she stretched with a crunch.

"Both of Olenka's titties are out."

Olga stood up. Seryozha threw her dressing gown and ran to the door.

"It's a serious question," she looked at the glans floating in the glass of water, "is Viktor up?"

"Olka's got a ginger cunt!"

Tossing her robe off to the side, Olga rushed over to him. He ducked out the door. Shoving the door open, she ran after him, caught up outside of the bathroom, deftly wrapped her arm around his back, squeezed his mouth shut with her hand, and pushed him into the bathroom with her bare knee.

"Now it's time to put some hair on your chest!"

Seryozha groaned. Olga undressed him, climbed into the bath with him, clamped his head between her thighs, and loudly slapped his thin, boyish buttocks.

"Seryozha Anishchenko has been prescribed a regimen of hydrotherapy."

"It's a serious question," she looked at the glans floating in the glass of water, "is Viktor up?"

She put the showerhead over Seryozha's buttocks and turned on the cold water. The water beat upon Seryozha's buttocks with a hiss. Seryozha squealed. Olga turned off the water.

"Do you want more or will you ask for forgiveness?"

"Forgiveness! Forgiveness!"

She let go of his head and, standing over him with the showerhead in hand, spread her long legs.

"Kiss it."

Down on his knees, Seryozha kissed her genitals, running his lips over her sparse pubic hair.

"More."

Seryozha kissed her genitals.

"Smack 'em."

Seryozha kissed them more, smacking his lips loudly.

"Oh, you little pig!" Olga grinned, grabbing him by the hair.

"What's the screaming for?" Rebrov walked naked into the bathroom.

"The baby's being baptized," Olga smiled. "How was thy rest?"

"Wonderful . . ." Rebrov walked over to the sink, looked at himself in the mirror, and ran a hand over his cheek.

Seryozha slid out of the bath, gathered his things, and left the bathroom, silent and offended. Olga turned on the cold water and the shower flowed over her.

"Mhmm . . . for, every great thing begins as a small one," Rebrov mumbled, took an electric razor from the shelf, and began to shave.

"Oy! Ach! Nice!" Olga shuddered beneath the water.

"Here's what I've been thinking. We're not going to call Kovshov ourselves. Let him sit and wait for our call. Then Naiman will go see the cooperators. With an ingot. And he'll start feeling around for Kovshov's udder."

"What d'you mean?" Olga turned off the shower.

"The cooperators have the radiotelephone. Get it?" Rebrov looked at her.

"Fantastic!" Olga shook her head and clapped her wet hands together. "Fantastic!"

"That's how we'll win."

Rebrov splashed cologne into the palm of his hand and quickly rubbed it over his cheeks.

They were eating breakfast in the orangery as usual.

"How are you feeling, Henry Ivanych?" Rebrov asked, stirring his coffee.

"Wonderfully," Shtaube was eating his eggs and ham with great appetite, "sleep is the best medicine. Avicenna was right."

"It doesn't hurt?"

"Absolutely not. Olga Vladimirovna, my darling, pour me another juice."

Olga stood up and began to pour orange juice into everyone's glasses from a crystal decanter. When she came to Seryozha, he covered his glass with his hand and grunted, "I won't have any."

Olga held out her left hand with her little finger outstretched. Seryozha paused, reluctantly held out his own, and linked it with Olga's.

"Make peace, make peace, all fighting you must cease," said Olga.

"If you wanna fight, then I'm gonna bite," Seryozha grumbled.

Olga kissed his head and poured him some juice. Rebrov finished his coffee and wiped his lips with a napkin.

"Friends. With your permission, I'm going to use this lull in the conversation to convey a little message. I didn't tell you yesterday, but I think that was for the best. The briquettes from Golubyov haven't arrived."

Olga froze with glass in hand. Shtaube stopped chewing.

"What . . . what do you mean?"

Rebrov shook his head.

"And Masha?" Olga put down her glass.

He shook his head again.

"But I don't understand, Viktor Valentinych!" Shtaube raised his voice. "Then how would you have us understand your pronouncements on Sunday? And Masha? Does this just mean we're just being led by the nose? I don't understand anything, explain it to me properly!"

Rebrov sighed.

"My dear Henry Ivanych. On Sunday, I was talking about the pedagogues. You should remember that."

"Yes! I do remember!" Shtaube squealed. "I remember! How you allowed . . . how you let that beast . . . that fucking bitch make a promise . . . She made a promise and you trusted her! How she laughed, how she agreed! The whore! And you, you interceded on Mishanya's behalf! You! You!" He stood up abruptly and clumsily, knocking over a glass of juice. "And I, I'm telling you! I'm telling you that I despise Mishanya! I shit on the Oryolians! I shit! I shit and piss on your exercises with them! I shit on that smelly money! Don't you see? They set a condition for us! They passed by a pair of blacks! Do-gooders! No!" he rapped his finger against the table. "You won't finish the third one! No, no! And I don't need any details! I don't need any tricks of the jaws! I'm not a clown, Viktor Valentinych! I'm not Naiman! Not that . . . that beast! That fucking! O-o-o! Scum!" Shtaube's face was pale and tears were glistening in his eyes. "I . . . I'm an old man! An old man! And do you think that I, an old man, should have to procure for this fucking . . . this motherfucking rat! Yes?! Me, a disabled, a sick individual?! I should appease Zlotnikov?! Go to the executive committee?! Play fetch for them?! Go for a ride with those bastards?! Yes?! Yes?! And the clods?! Yes? And the plates? Me?! And you've come to terms with this so easily? You?! You?!"

Rebrov raised his lowered head and began to speak quietly.

"I have the intermediate block."

Shtaube froze.

"What do you mean?"

"Since the fifteenth. It's with Tamara Alexeyevna."

Shtaube looked at Olga in confusion. She nodded.

"Well . . ." Shtaube shrugged, "then . . ."

He paused, staring fixedly at the table, then muttered, "Well . . . forgive an old man."

"Forget about it," Rebrov looked at his watch, "So we have the allotment at twelve. I ask that all of you be in a state of total readiness. And be more professional than last time. Tomorrow will be Operation No. 1. Please remember that. And about the inclined series."

"We won't forget," Shtaube put his napkin over the puddle of juice, sniffed the air, and bent down to Seryozha in the neighboring chair. "Bleh! You farted, didn't you?"

Seryozha's nose twitched in surprise.

"I . . . no . . ."

"He lets out a silent one and keeps his mouth shut! Right, Viktor Valentinych?"

Rebrov stood up.

"I'll be waiting for you at twelve."

They carried out the allotment in a small room next to Rebrov's office. They sat down in chairs placed at the four corners of a scan stretched out over the floor. Rebrov dropped a sphere of ebonite at its center. The sphere stopped at "joys." Olga covered her face with her hands.

"Don't worry," Rebrov smiled reassuringly.

Olga placed both plates on 6. Shtaube touched the red with the rod. Seryozha marked the "wall-bolt." Rebrov pulled on the second, moved the segment toward "horse," and touched the sphere. The sphere showed "dispersion."

Olga moved the left plate to 27. Shtaube passed by the yellow and the "bork" with the ring. Seryozha traced chalk along the "lighthouse-wall." Rebrov pulled on the 6 and the 9-cross, moved the segment to "marten," and touched the sphere. The sphere showed "trust." Olga moved the right plate to 18. Shtaube touched the blue with the rod and completed the loop. Seryozha erased the "wall-bolt" and marked the "wall-obstacle." Rebrov pulled on the 12, moved the segment onto the field, and touched the sphere. The sphere showed "agreement." Shtaube dropped the rod in frustration. Olga wept. Rebrov opened the book of lists and found the necessary page.

"9, 46, 21, 82, 93, 42, 71, 76, 84, 36, 71, 12, 44, 47, 90, 65, 55, 36, 426."

Shtaube spread his hands apart.

"Only the vaga, the stry, and the woop."

Rebrov nodded and closed the book. Olga wept violently.

"Should I leave?" Seryozha stood up from his chair.

Rebrov nodded. Seryozha left. Shtaube stood up and limped after him. Rebrov looked at Olga as she wept.

"Olga Vladimirovna, you'll have to . . ."

"I know! I know!" Olga sobbed.

Rebrov paused, picked up the sphere, the segment, and the rod, then walked out.

Before lunch, Rebrov and Shtaube were working on the first block while Olga and Seryozha were skiing in the woods. Having passed through three kilometers of fir trees, they stopped in a large clearing.

"Let's stop here," Olga looked around and stuck her poles into the snow.

Seryozha took off his small knapsack and started to untie it. Olga unbuttoned her jacket and took out a small sport pistol with a silencer.

"Hang them over there, one every ten steps."

"Ski steps?" Seryozha laughed, removing three kilograms of meat on hooks from the knapsack. "Those aren't steps, they're runs!"

"Okay, ten runs." Olga dropped her jacket into the snow and was left wearing only the USSR Olympic ski team uniform.

Seryozha set off and spent a long time hanging the pieces of meat from the lower branches of fir trees.

"Done!"

He skied back, stopped just behind Olga, and took out a stopwatch. The red meat sparkled in the sun against the green background. Olga pulled back the slide and began to quickly shoot at the meat. The meat swung back and forth on its hooks, shredding with every shot. Having emptied the clip, Olga inserted a new one and continued to shoot. She emptied clip after clip, continuing until the pieces of meat on the hooks had all disintegrated.

"How many?" she turned to Seryozha.

"Fifty . . . three."

She shook her head unhappily.

"Deplorable. I'll have to sway today."

"Can I try, Ol? Just three times?"

"It was made to fit my hand, darling. You won't be able to pull the trigger properly. You can try out a Makarov."

"Please Ol! Just once!"

"Okay, fine. Just make sure to grab it with both hands. Shoot at that spruce tree." Seryozha lifted up the pistol, aimed for a long time, then fired.

"Fantastic, you hit it. Let's see another."

He shot again and hit the tree. Shot again and missed.

"Don't worry, you'll do better with the Makarov," Olga took the pistol from him.

"This one's heavy."

"It's heavy. And it kicks like a horse. Shall we go to the river?"

"Mhmm."

Olga put on her jacket, Seryozha put on the knapsack. They began to walk together slowly.

"There's a ski trail there," said Olga. "But I think it's covered in snow."

"Does Rebrov have a big dick, Ol?" Seryozha asked.

"It's ordinary."

"Smaller than Farid's?"

"Of course. Hey, look!"

A squirrel jumped from a pine to a spruce. Bits of snow flew forth from the tree.

They ate at eight. After turkey with marinated fruits, Olga served chocolate mousse. The telephone rang. Rebrov picked up the receiver with its short antenna lying on a chair.

"Yes. Yes. Let them in."

He put down the receiver and scooped out a spoonful of mousse from the glass bowl.

"This is especially for you, Henry Ivanych."

"What?" Shtaube lifted his head.

"That was Viktor Afanasyevich Kartashov. He's coming to us in his Volga from the checkpoint."

"How? How? Hold on . . ." Shtaube coughed and dropped his spoon.

"He's probably coming with a gift."

"Hold on . . . my God . . ." Shtaube stood up, coughing. "How? What is this?"

"Calm down, Henry Ivanych. We won't give you up."

"Yes. Well, I . . ." Shtaube shrugged, now very pale.

"Go upstairs," Rebrov said calmly.

Shtaube took his cane and left the dining room.

"We'll meet in the hallway." Rebrov reached out for a cigarette and lit up. "Seryozha, bring me the brown briefcase from my office."

The boy left the room.

"Well, there," Rebrov looked at Olga with a smile. "Not all is lost."

"The support?" Olga asked.

"We won't need it."

The doorbell rang. Olga and Rebrov walked out into the hallway. Rebrov opened the door. A man of medium height wearing a grey puffy coat and a blue beanie stood in the threshold. He was holding a suitcase.

"Hullo." The man walked in and put the suitcase down onto the ground.

"Hello, Victor Afanasich," Rebrov pronounced dryly, closing the door behind Kartashov.

"I called at Odoyevsky, but there was no one there," Kartashov watched Seryozha descend the staircase.

Rebrov exhaled smoke, passed the cigarette to Olga, and took the briefcase from Seryozha. Kartashov sniffed and put his hands into the pockets of his coat.

Rebrov opened the suitcase, pulled out a metal object, and gave it to Kartashov.

"Mhmm," he took the object and quickly put it into his pocket.

"We'll call you," Rebrov opened the door.

"Mhmm. See you soon," Kartashov left, Rebrov locked the door, picked up the suitcase, and began to walk up the stairs. Olga and Seryozha walked after him. On the second floor, Shtaube was standing in the hall.

"Please, Henry Ivanych," Rebrov placed the suitcase in front of Shtaube.

Getting down onto his knee, Shtaube opened the suitcase. It was full of rumpled women's clothing and underwear.

"Well, well, well," Shtaube started to take the pieces of clothing out on the floor, quickly looking them over. There was a battered violin case under the clothing. Shtaube opened it. There was an oblong object wrapped in a plastic bag in the case. Shtaube unwrapped it and pulled out a woman's arm, clumsily severed at the elbow. There was a golden wedding ring on the hand's ring finger and the skin had been flayed from the little finger. Shtaube froze, looked at the arm, then dropped it into the suitcase, grabbed Rebrov's hand, and kissed it.

"You should be ashamed of yourself!" Rebrov pulled away and walked over to the stairs.

"Viktor Valentinych, my darling," Shtaube got up off of his knee.

"Tea, we'll drink tea," Rebrov began to walk down the stairs.

"Oy . . . my God," Shtaube wiped the sweat from his forehead.

"Do you want cognac or valerian?" Olga smiled.

"Me? I'll have some cognac, some cognac!"

Having shut themselves away in the billiard room, Rebrov and Shtaube were playing pyramid pool. Two six-candled chandeliers were lit and a half-finished bottle of Armenian cognac stood on a nightstand.

"The three just to the left of that side," Shtaube took aim and hit the ball, "whoo! I'll win your clothes right off . . . the nine in the middle."

"If you worked on the allotment like this, Henry Ivanych," Rebrov finished his cognac, "we'd already be halfway to Krasnoyarsk."

"Allotment, shallotment, here we go . . ." Shtaube hit the ball. "The fact that we've liquidated the carrion and infiltrated the party, old boy, is a matter of archival importance, as the baldie would say."

"By the way, I'm leaving the neighborhood committee workers in your care." Rebrov took the balls out of the pockets and placed them on the shelf. "If Gerasimov doesn't sub in, then our intermediate block won't be worth a single cent."

"He'll sub in, he has no choice," Shtaube looked at the table, rubbing his cue with chalk. "Gerasimov depends on Kovalenko, and Kovalenko depends on Bolshakov. And at any time of day we can just tell Bolshakov: hark, Sergei Sergeyich, we sing. Five and fourteen on the right."

"That's problematic," Rebrov muttered.

Shtaube missed.

"You always screw me up . . ."

"There's one more subtlety with Gerasimov . . . five on the right," Rebrov hit the ball and walked around the table. "Imagine it like this: you put pressure on Bolshakov through Kovalenko, he subs in, Gerasimov signs, and we get the disks. Tanya goes to Petersburg, Naiman and I call on the assholes, who agree to our terms and honestly carry out the restoration work, and just as sincerely . . . seven in the middle . . . they cough up Rybnikova's statements and immediately give them to Gerasimov, thus closing this vicious circle. And Gerasimov . . ."

"And Gerasimov puts Rybinkova's statement under his fat ass and is silent as a flatfish because Bolshakov doesn't just have the letter, but the almatra too."

"Are you sure?"

"I saw it with my own eyes."

"That changes things," Rebrov started to think.

"Changes things, changes thi-i-ings-s-s," Shtaube sang, bustling around the table, "the 'grandpa' by the side in the middle. Whoo! You're high and dry, Viktor Valentinych. Shall we finish the game?"

"No, thanks," Rebrov put down his cue. "When will you get in touch with Tanya?"

"How 'bout tomorrow," the old man poured himself more cognac, "right when we finish, I'll call. Or do you want me to now?"

"Call now," said Rebrov, looking at the candles.

At 9:25 in the morning, Rebrov pulled his car up to the entrance of the Oktyabrsky Military District commissariat building and maneuvered over to the curb.

"We'll call after the znedo," said Rebrov and opened the door. He was wearing the winter uniform of an air force lieutenant colonel and Olga was dressed in the uniform of a senior police lieutenant. Shtaube and Seryozha were wearing their usual clothing.

Rebrov and Olga got out of the car, went up the steps, and entered the building. The lieutenant on duty sitting behind a glass barrier stood up and saluted Rebrov, Rebrov returned his salute without stopping. They walked up to the second floor. The hallway was empty. Rebrov walked over to the chief of the military commissariat's office and opened the door.

"Hello," he said to the typing secretary.

"Hullo," she smiled back, "they're waiting for you in the Lenin Room."

"Got it," Rebrov shut the door and continued down the hallway.

Olga followed him. They entered the Lenin Room. Colonel Tkachenko, the chief of the military commissariat, was sitting at the head of a table covered over in a red tablecloth: Lieutenant Colonel Leshchinsky, Major Zubaryov, Major Dukhnin, Captain Korolyov, Captain Lomeyko, Captain Belyakov, Captain Terzibashyants, and Senior Lieutenant Volkov were all sitting at chairs around the table.

"Hello, comrades," Rebrov said cheerfully.

"Nikolai Nikolaich, welcome!" Tkachenko smiled as he stood up. They shook each other's hands. The officers stood up. Rebrov shook everyone's hand. Olga stood by the door.

"Come over here," Rebrov said to her coldly. She walked over and bowed her head.

"Introduce yourself," commanded Rebrov.

"Detective of the Kirov District Police Department in Moscow, Senior Police Lieutenant Svetlana Viktorovna Fokina."

"A-a-h . . . " Tkachenko walked over to her and put his hands behind his back. "So, that's who we are. And how old are we?"

"Twenty-six," Olga replied quietly.

"Not bad! Not bad at all!" Tkachenko frowned. "Twenty-six and twenty-six, what does that equal? Huh?"

"Fifty . . . two," she said in a barely audible tone.

"Fifty-two," he repeated, glaring at her viciously. "Open the door, Evgenii Stepanych."

Captain Korolyov walked over to a door opposite to the entrance, unlocked it, opened it, and began to walk down the stairs.

"After you," Tkacheko gestured with his head. Olga followed Korolyov down. The others followed her out. They went down the stairs and out into the courtyard of the military commissariat. There were several cars in the courtyard. Korolyov walked over to a greyish-blue minibus, opened the doors, and sat behind the wheel. Tkachenko sat in the passenger seat and the rest of them sat in the back.

"Let's go," Tkachenko nodded.

Korolyov started the car, drove out of the courtyard, and set off along Vavilov Street.

"What about Moiseyev, Nikolai Nikolaich?" Tkachenko asked without turning around.

"He's on a business trip," Rebrov replied.

"Well, too bad for him."

They turned onto Profsoyuznaya Street and were leaving Moscow within fifteen minutes. Profsoyuznaya Street became the Kaluga Highway and Korolyov began to drive faster. Thirty-six kilometers later, the minibus turned right off of the highway and set off along a straight, well-plowed road through the forest. After another two kilometers, the road came to a massive gate covered in red stars. Korolyov honked, the gate opened, the car started to move again, then stopped in front of a checkpoint made up of a single striped barrier. A soldier carrying an assault rifle approached. Tkachenko handed a paper and his certification to the soldier through the window. The soldier walked over to the checkpoint and then walked back to the car with a lieutenant. The lieutenant handed the certification back to Tkachenko and saluted him. The barrier went up and the car entered the perimeters.

"Go straight, then turn right near the barracks," Tkachenko said to Korolyov. They turned right near the barracks and stopped outside of a small two-story building.

"We're here," Tkachenko got out of the car, waited for the others to do the same, then was the first to enter the building. Rebrov, Olga, and the officers followed him in. In the building, there was a large elevator made up of two cabins guarded by three soldiers and an ensign. They saluted the officers, then the ensign pressed an elevator button and picked up the telephone.

"6, 23."

The doors of one cabin opened, the officers, Rebrov, and Olga went inside, the doors closed, and the cabin began to descend.

Tkachenko looked at Olga.

"You can't grease the palm of an iron soul."

Olga lowered her head.

"She cheated herself," Tkachenko grinned. "Give it here, mama!"

The officers smiled. The elevator stopped and the doors opened.

"After you," Tkachenko nodded and everyone walked out of the elevator into a huge basement room, lit by hundreds of neon lamps hanging from a high ceiling. The basement was empty, except for a group of soldiers visible in the distance.

"Forward!" Tkachenko ordered Olga. She slowly walked over to the soldiers. The others followed her.

"Faster!"

Olga began to walk faster. Having crossed the length of the basement, they approached the wall, half of which was steel-plated. Two soldiers with assault rifles were standing in front of the wall. A captain was sitting at a table with a phone on it. A stocky, grey-haired air force major general was standing by the table. Olga stopped when she was ten paces away from him. Everyone following her also stopped.

"What is it, no strength? Hmm?" the general asked. "Legs aren't working? Come on, come on, let's go!"

Olga walked up to him and stopped, lowering her head.

"What now? What next? Hmm?" he asked, looking Olga over.

Olga was silent.

"We're not talking? Hmm? You're already here, you know. Well, well!" he turned to the captain. "They deigned to make it here, Comrade Captain! You understand? Show 'em, let 'em have a look."

The captain picked up the phone.

"8, 43."

The steel part of the wall began to rise, revealing a dimly lit space. When the wall had disappeared into the ceiling, a huge tractor, intended for the transportation of medium-range SS-20 missiles, drove out of the space and into the basement. A huge bar of silvery-green metal was lying in the tractor bed. The tractor stopped.

"Well, well! Look at that!" the general shook his head. Olga lifted her head and looked at the bar.

"You bitch! You fucking bitch!" the general blurted out, screaming, and brought his pale face close to Olga's. "You thought you were smarter than everyone? Hmm? That you could fuck us around? Hmm? That you had the wool over our eyes? Yeah? You thought you could shove it down our throats and we'd gobble it down? Yeah? Do it, Pyotr Semyonich, do it! Whore! Fucking whore! She came crawling! The tattered bitch is right here! She thinks we'll swallow her shit! That we'll motherfucking swallow it! We'll shove it down her throat first! First! We'll just do it! Just do it like people do! Just do it, motherfucker! And I'll play the eight! Right?! Isn't that right, you bitch?! Right?! Hm?!"

He wound up and hit Olga in the face. She flew back, covered her face with her hands, and began to sob.

"Everything is permitted! You have permission! Yeah?! You can fuck people over, you can play dirty tricks! Go ahead and fuck 'em! Fuck 'em . . . I have the right! They'll eat it up no matter what! They can suck your clit, right? Right?! I shit and they eat it! They eat it! Well, not anymore, you cunt! Not anymore, bitch! You're gonna eat now! You! Seryozh!"

The captain picked up the phone.

"8, 12."

A siren sounded, the doors opened, and a group of soldiers carrying assault rifles ran in and began to form two lines. As soon as they were in position, the siren went quiet, and a command rang out.

"Alright squad, get in formation! Att-en-tion! Eyes to the right!"

The senior lieutenant walked over to the general with a sharp trot and brought his hand to his forehead in a salute.

"Comrade Major General, the second company is now assembled! The commander of the company is Senior Lieutenant Sevostyanov."

"Let's go then!" the general nodded to the captain.

The captain picked up the phone.

"8, the old woman."

The door opened and two soldiers wearing quilted jackets pushed an old woman wearing an old-fashioned dark-blue dress into the basement. She fell down with a groan, the soldiers grabbed her by the arms, dragged her along the floor, and dropped her next to Olga.

"Ninochka," the old woman groaned deliriously.

"No, no, no!" Olga fell to her knees and crawled over to the general. "Don't do it! I'm begging you! Have mercy! I'm begging you!"

"Yeah, cunt! Lost your nerve?!" the general kicked Olga with his boot. "Don't worry, it's time to cut loose! You'll see what I mean!"

"No! No!" Olga got up from the ground and ran toward the door, but the soldiers wearing quilted jackets caught up with her, knocked her down, and dragged her over to the general.

"Do we have your permission, Ivan Timofeyich?" Tkachenko walked over to Olga.

"Let's see it!"

Captain Korolyov grabbed Olga's left arm, Lieutenant Colonel Leshchinsky grabbed her right arm, and Tkachenko pulled back her hair.

"No! No!" Olga screamed.

"Why're you just sitting there, cunt?!" the general shouted at the old woman. "Come on! Take your clothes off! Show us your snatch! It's probably withered away! Have you been fucked at all in the last twenty years?! Well?!"

"No! No!" Olga struggled against the soldiers' grip.

"Oh God," the old woman moaned.

"Come on, get undressed, whore!" the general screamed. "Don't push me, bitch! Get 'em off! Get 'em off, cunt! I'm not gonna wait!"

The old woman started crying.

"What're you waiting for? C'mon!" the general screamed at the soldiers in their quilted jackets.

The soldiers began to pull the old woman's clothes off.

"No-o-o!" Olga let forth a prolonged scream.

"We'll give you a reason to say no! C'mon, then, bring the old bag over here so this one can sniff her snatch! C'mon!"

The soldiers wearing quilted jackets grabbed the naked old woman's arms, spread her legs apart, and brought her crotch to Olga's face. Olga reared back, but the officers pressed her face forward. Grabbing her hair, Tkachenko pressed her face insistently into the woman's genitals. Olga moaned.

"Sniff it! Sniff the cunt of the worthy pedagogue! Sniff! We haven't let her take a bath for a whole week and she smells sweet! Come on! Come on and sniff her some more!"

Tkachenko began to rub Olga's face in the old woman's genitals.

"There! There!" the general laughed. "Let 'er sniff her fill! Inhale! Inhale deeper! Now the ass! Stagnation also plays a role in there, as Gorbachev would say! She did one in her pants twice! Twice! The first time when they read the guilty verdict and the second time when she saw Erofeyev's ugly mug! That's right!"

The soldiers turned the old woman around and brought her thin, excrement-stained buttocks to Olga's face. Tkachenko began to rub Olga's face between the buttocks. Olga tried desperately to escape, but two more officers came to help the three already restraining Olga: Major Dukhnin and Captain Terzibashyants.

"Deeper! Deeper!" the general commanded. "The deeper you go, the tastier it gets!"

The old woman let out a shrill scream.

"And now let's see Comrade Fokina's mug! Show everyone!"

The officers turned Olga to face the soldiers. Her face was stained with feces.

"Bastard, bastard, bastard . . ." Olga sobbed. The old woman let forth a prolonged cry. Her legs, still spread apart, were shaking.

"And now we crush the pubic crab!" the general ordered.

The soldiers lifted the old woman into the air, then dropped her on the ground. She fell silent.

"One! Two! Three!" one of the soldiers ordered. Several of the soldiers jumped onto the old woman's back. Bones cracked and blood flowed from the old woman's mouth.

"I'll tell . . . I'll tell Basov . . . I . . . bastard," Olga wheezed.

"And now we need a specialist, Seryozh!"

The captain picked up the phone.

"8, Govorov."

Several minutes later, two soldiers and an ensign of the guard brought in a man dressed in an officer's uniform, but without épaulettes. They brought him over to the general and the ensign raised his hand up in salute.

"Comrade Major General, having been arrested on your orders, Govorov has now been brought to you."

"So, Nikolai Ivanych," the general lay his hands on his stomach with a smile. "How are you feeling? Was it very cold? Hmm?"

Govorov looked off to the side.

"Forgive me, Kolya," Olga moaned.

"He will certainly, certainly forgive you," the general said loudly and the officers laughed.

Govorov continued looking off to the side.

"Put him over there, ensign," the general nodded.

The ensign and the soldiers walked Govorov over to a column and began to tie him to it with ropes.

"What about the milk?" the general turned to the captain.

"In the fourth box, Comrade Major General."

"Well?"

The captain picked up the phone.

"8, milk from the fourth."

After tying him up, the soldiers and the ensign walked away from Govorov.

"Give the order," the general nodded.

"First column, on your knees!" the senior lieutenant commanded.

"Sniff it! Sniff the cunt of the worthy pedagogue! Sniff! We haven't let her take a bath for a whole week and she smells sweet! Come on! Come on and sniff her some more!"

"Deeper! Deeper!" the general commanded. "The deeper you go, the tastier it gets!"

The soldiers in the first column got down onto their right knees.

"Kolya! Kolya!" Olga screamed. "No! Bastards! You bastards!"

Tkachenko picked up the old woman's torn dress and stuffed its sleeve into Olga's mouth.

"Weapons at the ready."

The soldiers pulled back their operating rods.

"A short round into the head of the Traitor of the Motherland. Fire!" the senior lieutenant dropped his hand.

The sound of 110 assault rifles rumbled through the air. Gorovov's head exploded into little pieces. The body, tied by its hands to the column, tilted forward and blood flowed from its tattered neck.

"First column, stand up! Guns-at-your-shoulders-men!!"

Two soldiers wheeled in a wide cart with twenty pails of milk on it from the dimly lit hangar.

"So," the general looked at the cart, then at the captain. "And now?"

The soldiers brought the cart to a halt in front of the tractor. The captain stood up, walked over to the cart, opened a pail, bent over, and sniffed the milk. Everyone was looking at him. He straightened up and looked at the general. The general looked down and sighed heavily. Then walked slowly over to Olga and squatted down. Tkachenko liberated her mouth.

"You understand," the general began, "if there is no trust or certainty that you can rely on someone, then everything loses its meaning. Everything. But, on the other hand, offending someone with your lack of trust and, so to speak, keeping them at a distance can also alienate them. Can alienate them forever. That's the problem. I hate that idiotic expression: 'trust but verify.' Stalinist apparatchiks and careerists thought it up while they were wading through corpses. It was important for them to pull the people apart and to sow suspicion and uncertainty into their work, into their very being. Which meant depriving them of their professional pride, separating them from their preferred occupations, dragging them into the swamp of factory squabbles, and turning them into pawns in, so to speak, partocratic games. As a consequence, their personhood was destroyed. Which is to say, speaking in simple terms, this deprived them of the title of Man."

He went quiet and looked down at his wrinkled hands.

"Ivan Timofeyich," Tkachenko began cautiously, "Sergei Anatolyich and I would like to clarify what's going on in Podolsk. They called yesterday and today. Basov's not there and I can't get a report regarding Panchenko."

"Why?" the general raised his head.

"I can't," Tkachenko shook his head.

"Comrade Colonel, you need to push through this 'I can't,'" the general stood up. "Seryozh, call Klokov."

The captain picked up the phone.

"3, 16. Comrade Colonel, this is Captain Chervinsky. Colonel Tkachenko has just come here with Fokina. Yes. Yes. On the ninth. Ivan Timofeyich?" the captain looked inquisitively at the general, who waved his hand. "He already left. Yes. Already rolled out. Yes. Sir yes sir, Comrade Colonel."

"Well then," the general looked at his watch. "That means I'll head back to mine. Not a peep to Klokov about the tricine. Let *him* fuckin' hustle."

The general walked over to the nearest door and disappeared through it. Olga struggled against the grip of the officers still holding her.

"Let her go," commanded Tkachenko. And they did. Olga got up off of her knees, walked over to the open pail of milk, and began to wash her face. At the other end of the basement, the elevator doors opened and Colonel Klokov walked out.

"No one tells him anything, got it?" Tkachenko said quietly, then turned to meet Klokov. They saluted each other and shook hands.

"Squad! Get in formation! Attention!" commanded Sevostyanov. "Eyes to the center!"

"Alright, at ease," Klokov said and walked over to the officers. "Hello, comrades."

The officers greeted him.

"What's the situation?" he looked at the old woman's blood-slick corpse and at Govorov's headless body.

"It's become more warlike!" Tkachenko replied and everyone laughed.

"Very good," Klokov saw Olga, who was cleaning her face with a handkerchief. "Comrade Fokina! Where's your teammate? Captain Vorontsov? Our wonderful investigator?"

Olga didn't reply.

"Did something happen?"

Olga put away the handkerchief and straightened her tunic.

"The statement is in Major Zubaryov's pocket."

The officers turned to Zubaryov. For a moment, he looked at Olga, then turned to run for the door, but Rebrov stuck out his leg to trip him. Zubaryov fell down and everyone jumped on top of him, pushing him to the floor.

"Turn him over," commanded Klokov, as he approached.

They flipped Zubaryov over.

"Search him."

The officers searched him and took a folded piece of paper out from the inside pocket of his tunic. Klokov unfolded it and began to read. Olga walked over and looked at the paper.

"Yes. Lisovsky's handwriting. And look at the loops down a little lower. Oguryeyev's."

Klokov tightened his lips and nodded. Olga handed him a lighter. He accepted it.

"Senior Lieutenant Sevostyanov!"

Sevostyanov walked over to them.

"Ask this dumbass where the samples are. And if he won't say, then put a bullet through his forehead."

Sevostyanov took his pistol out of its holster, pulled back the slide, and pointed it at Zubaryov. .

"They're in the safe . . . over at Zhoglenko's . . ." Zubaryov mumbled.

Klokov clicked the lighter and lit the paper.

"Fire."

Sevostyanov fired. The bullet entered Zubaryov's chest, he moaned, arching his back. The officers let go of him. Klokov dropped the burning paper onto the floor and handed the lighter to Olga.

"Thank you. Lieutenant, give me two soldiers."

"Sobolevsky, Ahmetyev, come forward!" commanded Sevostyanov and the soldiers walked over to the colonel.

"You come too," Klokov said to two soldiers wearing quilted jackets. "Follow me. March."

He headed for the elevators. Rebrov, Olga, and the soldiers followed him.

"Back in Podolsk, he assured me that we'd nail the parameters on our first try," Klokov said as they walked. "We were examined by the commission and by GUT, we checked in with Yazov, left for Barnaul, but he just got more and more worried and kept writing reports. To Basov, to Polovinkin, and to that asshole Vashchenko: the normal quotas weren't being met, the object had been handed over before it was completed, the barsovites were leaking, the magneto was flowing, and there was a breakdown in the output."

They got into the elevator, he pressed button 3 and continued.

"And then, in September, two weeks of rain, the roads fall apart, there're as many tractors as I've got flippers, the power engineers scream their heads off at us, we get put in the 572nd, the commission howls, Leska Gobzev gets dismissed, Basov flips out, Ivan Timofeyich and I are stretched thin . . ."

The elevator stopped and the doors opened. Klokov was the first to step out onto the roll of carpet leading down the hall.

"And, suddenly, this bastard comes up to me and shows me a photo. When I'd just had a conversation with Basov. That was when I started to feel some doubt . . ."

They walked over to a door numbered 35. Klokov opened it and was the first to walk through.

An ensign sitting at a table stood up.

"Back to work, back to work," Klokov waved his hand, walked over to the black upholstered door, and opened it. "Those of you with assault rifles—stay here."

The soldiers with assault rifles stood by the door and the others walked into a comfortable, oak-paneled office. Klokov shut the door behind them and made a command.

"One!"

A soldier in a quilted jacket kicked Rebrov in the stomach and another bent back Olga's arm. Rebrov keeled over and collapsed onto the floor. Olga fell to her knees.

"That's right," Klokov walked over to the safe, unlocked the outer door with a key, and dialed a combination lock to open the inner door. "Don't set a wolf to watch sheep . . ."

"What? Why are you doing this?!" Olga cried, grimacing with pain.

"Give him another one," Klokov took a red folder out of the safe.

A soldier kicked Rebrov in the back with his boot.

"Any questions?" Klokov walked over to Rebrov. "Or is everything clear?"

"Everything's . . . clear," Rebrov croaked.

"Replacement number?"

"28, row 64 . . ."

"Which band?"

"The eighth."

"Good," Klokov opened the folder and took out a piece of paper. "Thus, instead of a well-deserved bullet through your forehead, you are to receive the samples. Today, in the sixth depot, by consignment. Stand up."

Rebrov stood up with some difficulty.

"Here," Klokov handed him the piece of paper. Rebrov took it and, frowning, began to read.

"Let her go," Klokov said to the soldier holding Olga, who then let go of her arm and helped her to stand up.

"Now, go up the stairs," Klokov pressed a button, an oak panel shifted off to the side, and a passage opened up in the wall, "shut the door behind you. My chauffeur is waiting with a car by the infirmary."

Olga was the first to go through the opening.

"And, as a parting gift from all personnel," Klokov slapped Rebrov violently across the face. "See what happens if I catch you again, shit-ass! Get outta here!" He kicked Rebrov. Rebrov shuffled through the opening and the panel closed behind him. Dim lamps burned in the passageway and a spiral staircase wound upward. Olga embraced Rebrov rapturously.

"Oy, Vitya! Vitenka!"

"It's too early," he whispered, moving away from her. "Let's move . . ."

They walked up the staircase, opened an iron door, and found themselves in a boiler room.

"Where's the . . ." Rebrov turned his head. "Aha. There's the infirmary."

"Hold on, you've got a busted lip," Olga took out a handkerchief and wiped away the blood.

"Come on, let's go," Rebrov walked quickly over to the infirmary.

"Vitya! Vitenka!" Olga caught up to him. "You're a fucking mess! Oy! Baby . . . does it hurt a lot?"

"Be quiet."

They walked past a group of soldiers leaving the canteen and walked over to the infirmary. There was a black Volga parked nearby. Rebrov sat down in the passenger seat and Olga in the back seat.

"Good day, Comrade Lieutenant Colonel," the sergeant sitting behind the wheel started the engine.

"Yo," Rebrov touched his lip. "Moscow, Dorogomilovskaya, Number 42."

"Yessir, Comrade Lieutenant Colonel," the sergeant shifted into gear and the car started to move.

"What do you mean Dorogomilovskaya?" Olga leaned forward in shock. "Why?"

Rebrov looked at her sternly.

"I can't! I won't! Oh God!" she put her hands over her face.

"The Volga flows into the Caspian Sea," Rebrov said drily.

They sat in silence. On Bolshaya Dorogomilovskaya, they turned into a courtyard and stopped . . .

"Wait here," Rebrov told the driver, quickly got out of the car, and opened the door to the back seat. "Please."

Olga got out of the car and stumbled over to the building's entrance. She began sobbing in the elevator.

"Olga Vladimirovna, I'm begging you," Rebrov took her by the hand, "I'm really begging you."

"But why! Why am I . . . My God, I can't!" she shook her head. "It was all going so well . . . I mean, why?!"

"You understand absolutely everything, darling, you remember 18 in the allotment, it's difficult for me too, but we're on our way, and then it'll be so easy to make a clean break and destroy everything. Pull yourself together, I'm begging you, don't screw us over. We can't afford to relax. To relax means to die and to take others with you. Well!" he shook her by the shoulders.

"Yes, yes," Olga sobbed, pulling out a handkerchief, "to die . . ."

They got out of the elevator, she wiped her face, and Rebrov rang the bell for apartment 165.

"I'm not giving you orders, I'm asking you nicely," he said. Ivanilov opened the door. He was wearing a flannel shirt, long underwear, and slippers on his bare feet.

"At just precisely the right moment," he smiled, letting them into the narrow entranceway. "And I . . . this . . . they're showing the congress on there, and Yeltsin is really giving it to 'em . . ." Noise from a television filled the apartment. "They're climbin' all over him, y'see, and he just knocks 'em down! Woah, woah . . . Polozkov's people! Can I get you some tea?"

"We're in a hurry, Pyotr Fyodorovich," Rebrov said dryly, unbuttoning Olga's overcoat.

"You know best." Ivanilov turned off the television and opened a drawer in his bureau. Rebrov hung Olga's overcoat on a coatrack, she took off her fur hat and went into the small adjoining room. Ivanilov took a grey folder out of the bureau and put it on the table.

"Be a little neater this time, Pyotr Fyodorovich," Rebrov walked into the kitchen and looked out the window. "We've had an incredibly difficult day."

"I got it." Ivanilov walked into the adjoining room with a smile on his face and locked the door behind him. The room's window was occluded by tightly drawn curtains. Sitting on a narrow bed in the corner, Olga took off her boots. In the middle of the room sat an old dentist's chair, above which a chair with a round hole in its bottom was fastened to a table. Ivanilov quickly got undressed and put his clothes on the edge of the bed.

"Let me give you a hand, Svetlana Viktorovna."

"Get away from me!" Olga shook her head. He walked away and over to the chair, stroking his shoulders. She got undressed and sat down in the dentist's chair. With his back to Olga, Ivanilov climbed up onto the table and sat down on the chair fastened to it. He positioned his buttocks over the hole, which hovered directly over Olga's face.

"Just go slowly," Olga said, gripping on to the armrests firmly.

"Stands to reason . . ." Ivanilov tensed up, letting forth a protracted and noisy jet of gas into Olga's face. She opened her mouth and put it to his anus. Ivanilov began to slowly defecate into Olga's mouth, grunting quietly. Olga swallowed his feces convulsively, inhaling frantically through her nose. Her bare legs trembled.

"That's all," mumbled Ivanilov, getting back up. Olga slid down from the dentist's chair and onto the floor, then became completely immobile, sobbing and breathing loudly.

"That's all, that's all," Ivanilov got down from the table and onto the floor, then started to get dressed. "Which segment?"

Olga didn't reply.

"Well, then I'll just . . ." he finished getting dressed and left the room.

Rebrov was drinking milk in the kitchen.

"Which segment is it?" Ivanilov asked loudly. Rebrov put down his glass and walked into the room.

"The eighteenth."

"M'kay. The eighteenth." Ivanilov rustled through the segment file in the bureau and pulled out an outline.

"Please make two copies."

"Got it, got it."

Ivanilov took two charts out of the folder, laid the outline over them, and traced around it.

Olga came in, buttoning up her overcoat.

"You okay?" Rebrov walked over to her.

She shook her head. He took out a handkerchief and wiped the brown off of her lips.

"Everything'll be alright."

"Done," Ivanilov put away the outline and the folder and immediately turned the television back on. "I wonder if he'll get the property stuff through . . ."

Olga went to put her coat on. Rebrov picked up the charts, folded them, and put them into his pocket.

"On the other hand, you need to understand collective farmers too," Ivanilov laughed. "They worked, they worked, and then suddenly: 'screw you!' You see what I mean?"

"Goodbye, Pyotr Fyodorovich," Rebrov said and he and Olga left. Olga vomited in the elevator.

"It's the easiest thing of all! It's the easiest thing of all to give free rein to egoism!" Rebrov exclaimed. "Come on! Show me how proud you are! How independent you are! Show me! How much disdain you have for the world around you! How you couldn't give a damn about anyone but yourself! Come on! Show me!"

"I . . . no . . ." Olga whispered, pressing her forehead against the wall of the elevator.

Rebrov grabbed her by the elbow and forced her out of the elevator.

"Let's go! Have a little pride!"

They got into the car.

"We're going to the sixth depot," said Rebrov, lighting a cigarette.

"Yessir, Comrade Lieutenant Colonel."

When the black Volga drove up to the military enlistment office, it was already dark outside. Rebrov's car was parked in front of the office. Shtaube and Seryozha were sleeping inside of it, leaning against each other as they did.

"Load my trunk and then you're free to go," Rebrov ordered the sergeant as he got out of the Volga. Olga knocked on the back window of the Zhiguli.

"Hey!"

Shtaube woke up, opened the door, and Olga sat in the front seat.

"Good morning, sweethearts."

"How'd it go?" asked Shtaube, frowning.

"Wonderfully!" she whispered joyfully. "Look over there."

Shtaube looked around. The sergeant brought a metal box over to the Zhiguli.

"Thank God."

Rebrov shut the trunk and sat down behind the wheel.

"Good day, Henry Ivanych."

"Did they give it to you? 48?"

"They gave me 48," Rebrov started the engine. "You didn't get too cold in here?"

"I started the car twice. Hold on—how was it with Klokov? And what about Basov? Did they find the statement right away?"

"Right away!" Rebrov looked at Olga and they started laughing. "Right away!"

"And did that little shit Sotnikov try to haggle with you?"

Rebrov and Olga laughed even harder.

"Hold on, what're you laughing for? Tell me everything! Should I go to Kovalenko?"

Seryozha woke up and yawned loudly.

"A-a-agh . . . it's chilly . . . where's Olka?"

"I'm here, sweetie. Sleep."

"I want something to eat."

"Yes," Rebrov became more serious, "food. We all need to have some lunch. Or it's dinnertime, I guess."

"Shall we go to Mikhas's?" Olga suggested. "I've got a terrible urge to be in a banya."

"Go to Mikhas's? Without calling?" Rebrov rubbed his forehead.

"Precisely without calling!" Shtaube put on his hat. "That bastard should be licking your balls day and night! Without cease! Let's go."

They were sitting at a table in an empty bathhouse with marble columns and a pool. Rebrov and Shtaube were wrapped in sheets and Olga and Seryozha were naked. A waiter brought them dessert and champagne.

"To success," muttered Rebrov, less tense now. They clinked their glasses and drank.

"Motherfucker . . ." Shtaube frowned and picked up the bottle. "Semi-sweet. The tasteless cunts. Waiter!"

The waiter walked over.

"What is this shit you brought us? Who the fuck said we wanted it semi-sweet? Do you not have any decent champagne?"

"I'm sorry, but they only delivered semi-sweet."

"Motherfucker!" Shtaube slammed the bottle down on the table. "Get Mikhas out here!"

"Just a minute . . ."

"Everything's okay, Henry Ivanych," Olga finished her champagne, stood up, and got into the pool. "Seryozh, c'm'ere!"

Seryozha jumped into the water.

"Doing that . . . after eating . . . it's unhealthy!" Shtaube shook his finger at them.

"It's wonderful!" Olga cried out.

"Give her syrup with water and she'll say that's wonderful too," Shtaube muttered, taking a bite of an apple.

Olga grabbed Seryozha's hand and pulled him out into the middle of the pool.

Seryozha squealed. Mikhas walked in.

"My dear friend . . . what the hell is this?" Shtaube flicked the bottle.

"Forgive me, Mikhail Abramych, for the love of God!" Mikhas pressed his plump palm to his chest. "It's really hard to get brut right now, all of it goes to foreign-currency bars and we don't get any. Do you want some Napareuli? A gin and tonic? I have a nice lil' liqueur. An egg liqueur."

"An egg liqueur?" Shtaube narrowed his eyes mockingly. "You're dogshit! Don't you see who's come to pay you a visit?! You're a stupid cunt with your head up your ass! Who do you think we are? District-committee hookers? Your henchmen? *Who* could possibly lap up this rot-gut? What are we to you, bastard? Answer me!" he pounded his fist on the table, knocking the champagne glasses over.

"Henry Ivanych," Rebrov, now drunk, lifted his hand, "no need for that . . . they're all just . . . your subordinates."

"Excuse me, forgive me, please, I'll bring you everything we have, everything we have!" Mikhas mumbled.

"Bring it all, bastard! Everything! Bring it all right here! Everything!" Shtaube pounded his fist. "Semi-sweet! Did you not eat enough sugar when you were a kid, you little shit?! Or did you think we were blockade-niks? Or that we were veterans, fuck their bald skulls?! You better give 'em an enema with this semi-sweet champagne, got it?! Stick it right up their hemorrhoidal anuses! Got it? But not us! You can shove this . . ." he picked up the bottle and threw it at Mikhas, "up your ass!"

Mikhas jumped over to the side and the bottle broke against one of the columns.

"Bravo!" Olga slapped her palms against the surface of the water.

"Hooray!" Seryozha yelled, hanging from her neck. Mikhas slid out the door.

"Such animals!" Shtaube shook his head. "Hang them all with one rope! All of 'em!"

"Henry Ivanych, you're far too categorical," Rebrov opened Olga's cigarette case and pulled one out. "You . . . or no . . . we are dealing with the simplest of beings, with, you know, infusoria, with *Amoeba proteus*, which always become food for more complex creations, crustaceans eat them, for example, and then whales eat the crustaceans and then . . . then killer whales attack the whales, rip apart their mouths, pull out their fat, fat tongues, and then bipedal mammals catch the killer whales, while parasites and insects are attacking them. So, it must be said, the distance separating infusoria from lice is enormous. Let's have some more vodka."

"Viktor Valentinych!" Shtaube tossed away his half-eaten apple, "you'll have to forgive me, in terms of allotment and znedo, you're a genius, but when it comes to real life, you don't understand anything! Those infusoria drive around in Mercedes sedans! Whores from the district committee and even the executive district committee suck 'em off continuously! We should hang these stupid cunts up by the balls so that they piss and shit at the same time! Infusoria! Shit-suckers! Fuckin' ball-breakers! How I hate those fat-lipped animals! I ha-a-ate them!" he pounded his fist on the table.

"Vitya! Henry Ivanych! Come join us!" Olga yelled. "That's enough swearing!"

"Not a bad idea, I'd say," Rebrov lit a cigarette and dropped the match into the pool. "Shall we give in to temptation, Henry Ivanych?"

"Animals! Fucking animals!" Shtaube sloppily poured vodka for himself and Rebrov.

"You've had enough," Rebrov took his glass. "Success, success. Three days ago . . . I was getting ready to call it quits. Let's drink to the intermediate block."

They drank.

"Ha-HA!" Shtaube yelled, bit into a lemon, and started to chew.

"Help me! I'm dro-o-o-wwwwning!" cried Seryozha, grabbing on to Olga's neck.

"Get off, pussycat," Olga laughed, pushing him away. "Swim, darling, swim! Grip on to the water!"

Rebrov stood up, staggered to the edge of the pool, threw off his sheet, and plopped into the water with the cigarette still between his teeth.

"All the poor children in the forest, who will show them the way?" Shtaube spat out the lemon, stood up, and began jumping up and down, his stump spinning round and round. "I shall carry forth their lamenting cry . . . carry it quietly to the threshold of my home . . . The animals!" he fell, crawled to the corner of the pool, then sat up, dangling one foot into the water. "That's how life passes you by . . ."

Rebrov went under the surface of the water and came back up snorting.

"Chlorine . . ."

Mikhas appeared pushing a trolley of bottles. A full-figured girl with flowing hair in a long dress carrying a guitar followed him in.

"Well, now that's what I'm talkin' about!" Shtaube grinned, scratching his chest. "Pour me somethin'."

"What would you like?"

"I don't care. Who's that?"

"That's Natasha, Mikhail Abramych. She sings enchantingly well. She sang for you that one time, don't you remember?"

The girl smiled and began to strum.

"A-a-a-a-h," Shtaube frowned, accepting a glass of liquor. "I remember now. 'I dreamt of a garden wreathed in wedding crown.' But it won't do the trick today. Your voice sounds like ass hair, darling: it's fine and it's thin, but it sure ain't clean. And my hearing aids are delicate things. Back in '57, I almost spat in Kozlovsky's face—you're really risking your pretty face if you think you're any better. So . . ." he took a sip from his glass, "drop your bandura, get yourself a glass of something, and crawl on over to me. You! Pour her something!"

Mikhas poured a glass of wine and gave it to Natasha.

"And get the fuck out of here while I'm still feelin' nice!"

"Then who will serve us?" Olga cried out. "I want wine too!"

"Me three!" Seryozha yelled.

The swimmers moved to the edge of the pool and Mikhas began to serve them.

Natasha walked over to Shtaube with a glass in her hand.

"Take your clothes off and sit down!" he slapped his palm against the wet floor. She took off her dress and shoes and, wearing only a red bathing suit, sat down next to Shtaube, dangling her feet in the water.

"That's not gonna cut it!" Shtaube smirked. "We're in Eden here, you see how we're dressed . . ." he took off his sheet and scratched his scrotum. "So, don't spoil the mood, that's the second thing. And the first thing is I already told you to have a drink!"

He grabbed Natasha by the neck with his left hand, brought the glass to her lips with his right, and forced her to drink.

"Oy . . . I can't breathe!" Natasha sputtered.

"Now, that's another story!"

Shtaube started to take off Natasha's swimsuit and she helped him.

"Look at you!" he touched her large breasts. "Hey guys! Look!"

"How lovely!" Olga laughed, taking a sip from her glass.

"Show us your pussy!" Seryozha growled in a basso tone.

Shtaube spread Natasha's legs apart.

"Have a look! You like it?"

"V-eer-y much!" Seryozha growled, sipping his wine.

"Are you turned on, Vitya?" Olga hugged Rebrov.

"I'm sluggish with success . . ." he laid his head down on a marble step.

"Then who's gonna do it?!" Olga slapped her hand against the water. "Henry Ivanych hasn't had an erection in five years!"

"Six!" Shtaube corrected her and showed Olga his long member. "See what I was working with? Twenty-six centimeters in its full glory! But that's all in the past. Now . . ."

"Now, who's gonna fuck her?!" Olga shouted, splashing around in the water.

"Let him do it!" Seryozha pointed at Mikhas scrambling around with the bottles.

"Great!" Shtaube clapped his hands. "Well now, cocksucker, get those clothes off!"

"What do you mean . . . why me?"

"Don't argue with me, pussy! Do as you're told!"

Mikhas began to reluctantly take off his clothes.

"I'm not gonna do it with him!" Natasha shook her head.

"Oh, you will!" Shtaube grabbed her by the hair. "You're gonna suck him off with that juicy little mouth, swallow what comes out, and then say thank you!"

"I'm not gonna!" Natasha pulled away from him.

"You will! You will! You will!"

Shtaube began to slap her across the face. She started to sob.

"Get on your knees, slut!" Shtaube pushed her over to Mikhas, who was now naked. "Suck him off! With some pizzazz! I'm not gonna repeat myself, little miss cunt! Well!" He waved the bottle, spilling the liquor.

Sobbing, Natasha got down onto her knees. Mikhas walked up to her and she began to suck his penis.

"That's more like it," Shtaube took a sip from the bottle.

"Some dudes are just too hairy," Olga laughed.

"Does she like the taste?" Seryozha threw a mandarin rind at Natasha.

"You bet!" Shtaube nodded seriously.

The waiter came in with ice cream.

"Put it there . . ." Mikhas muttered.

"Give it to me! To me!" Seryozha yelled.

"To me too!" Olga raised her hand.

"And me," Rebrov sighed wearily.

"And me!" Shtaube stretched out.

The waiter distributed the ice cream and left.

"Now, that's another story . . ." Shtaube splashed liqueur into the dish of ice cream and tasted it, "I recommend you eat it like this."

Olga and Seryozha swam over to him, Shtaube poured them liqueur, then looked at Mikhas and Natasha.

"Don't get distracted, friends. Show us your Kotovsky, Mikhas."

Natasha moved away from Mikhas, who turned around, showing everyone his penis.

"Not a bad banana!" Olga chuckled drunkenly.

"Is Farid's smaller?" Seryozha pinched at her breasts.

"A very respectable bit of buckwheat!" Shtaube nodded. "Well done! Now let's see you do it doggy-style! Come on now!"

Resting on her knees, Natasha bent over and Mikhas entered her from behind.

"A little more lively!" Olga prompted.

"What?" Rebrov lifted his head. "Stop! Stop! Quickly! Quickly!"

He climbed awkwardly out of the pool, slipped, and fell down onto his side.

"Quickly! The rings! Get them out of here! Out!"

"Get out! Get out!" Shtaube shouted. "Step on it! Or I'll kill you!"

Mikhas and Natasha picked up their clothes and ran out of the room.

"What's going on? Vitya?" Olga got out of the pool.

"The rings! The rings!" Rebrov crawled over to the box in the corner.

"What rings?" Shtaube followed him, pulling himself along the floor and dragging his leg behind him.

Rebrov entered the combination into the lock, opened the box, took out the eequest, pulled the transverse-supply lever, and started to laugh.

"What's wrong?" Shtaube looked into the box.

"I thought . . . that I'd forgotten to take the rings . . ."

"You're exhausted, Vitya. It's gotten to you," Olga kissed him on the shoulder.

"It happens . . ." Shtaube crawled away.

"You need to get some sleep," Olga stroked Rebrov's wet head, "let's go upstairs? Sleepy time?"

"Upstairs?" he rested his head on her shoulder. "Let's move . . . but the box, the box stays with me . . . stays with me . . . next to me so that . . ."

"Of course, darling."

They made it back to the dacha at around two in the afternoon. Olga and Seryozha went to the gym. Rebrov and Shtaube—to the workshop. Shtaube immediately carved a half-ring in the lathe and measured the key.

"It's up to code."

Rebrov opened the box, took out the eequest, turned the transverse-supply lever, and carefully pulled rod no. 1 out of its groove.

"Well done!" Shtaube shook his head enthusiastically. "The bastards know how to do what needs to be done!"

Rebrov put the ring onto the lever, inserted the half-ring, and pulled the spring. The bolt snapped and fell into place. Rebrov reinserted the rod into its groove, secured the lever, moved the pole to 9, and extended his hand to Shtaube. Shtaube handed him the gnek. Rebrov inserted it into the slotted lock and began to turn it slowly.

"Gently, gently!" whispered Shtaube.

Rebrov turned the gnek to the end; the telmets leaped off of the pad and entered the shuttle pod. Shtaube handed him the needle. Rebrov inserted it into the end hole and turned the pole to 2. The shuttle capsule dropped onto the paraclete. Rebrov immediately turned and pulled out the gnek.

"Praise be to you, oh Lord!" Shtaube crossed himself and clutched at his heart with a sigh. "Oy . . . With tricks like these, you're gonna put me in the ground, Viktor Valentinych . . ."

"Wonderful! Wonderful!" Rebrov walked over to the intermediate block, opened it, inserted the circuit breaker, inserted the gnek into the cartridge, and turned it on. The gnek twisted around, opened up along its crown, and the tungsten ball disappeared into the branch pipe.

"This is what they turn our people's money into," Shtaube leaned over the box. "Bastards! And they still can't figure out how to make a decent prosthesis."

"Everything's terrific, Henry Ivanych!" Rebrov excitedly pulled rod no. 2 out of its groove. "Let's just deal with the fundaments. Everything will come with time, even a new prosthesis. Carve the half-ring."

Olga climbed down from the exercise machine and rubbed her back.

"The third sweat. Enough. Turn it off, Seryozha."

Seryozha was pedaling on the Delta.

"But I want to go on the Hercules too, Ol!"

"Stop! Stop! You're still too young. A Swedish wall, skis, rings . . . That's what you need. Get down."

Olga touched his back.

"You're soaked through. Three minutes with the jump rope and then a shower!"

After they were done jumping, they went into the shower room, got undressed, and stood under the streams of water.

"And what happened after that? After the USSR Championship?" Seryozha asked, continuing their conversation.

"There was a scandal. I crossed paths with the great Strepetova. She was a six-time national champion, a two-time world champion, an Olympic champion, and I was just a twenty-year-old chick who'd earned her normal sports certification a year earlier. Her husband was in the KGB, they had a dacha, two cars, and a handy connection in the government sports committee. And I was a girl from Norilsk, a third-year student at an atrocious forestry institute, I was living in a dorm, I didn't know anyone in Moscow, my whole life: shooting range, gym, dorm, shooting range, gym, forestry institute. Then things got cooler: at the Spartakiad of the Peoples of the USSR, right before the Olympics, she shoots a 559. I go out: 564! A new national record. Everyone in the Federation gets their hackles up. Danilin: Pestretsova must be on the Olympic team. Komarov: it's too early, she's still young, she has no experience, has no affiliation with the Komsomol, she'll let down the team, she's morally unstable, and so fuckin' on and forth. The vote was split and they decided to wait for a week. Strepetova went into hysterics in front of Komarov and yelled, 'it's either her or me!' Her panties were in a twist at that point: she was twenty-nine, well past her peak, and, at the last world championship, Angelica Forster had shit all over her, so badly that she wasn't even in the top three in Rome . . ." Olga turned off the water and pulled out a towel. "So. That was the situation. A week passes, they have to make a decision, and I've given up, it's all frickin' over: she's got Komarov's ear, he'll convince the Federation, they'll vote against me, and I'm fucked. And then, Milka Radkevich comes from Kiev, we go to Blizzard Queen, get a little drink, shoot the shit, and she says to me, 'stop screwin' around, Olenka, get a bottle of cognac and take it over to Zhabin's.'"

"Who's that?" Seryozha turned off the water.

"The second-most eminent person in the Federation after Komarov. A ghastly womanizer, Milka told me everything about him. When he was coaching the Leningrad Dynamo squad, he fucked the whole team. Well, back then I was very driven and, whenever I thought about the Olympics, my heart would skip a beat. I thought that if I didn't get put on the national team I'd throw in the fucking towel, move out to the countryside, and become a gym teacher. I call Zhabin: I say this and that, blah blah frickin' blah, Viktor Sergeyich, I want to consult with you. He didn't catch on at first: but can't Danilin help out with this? I say, 'as a trainer, Danilin is fantastic, but as a man, well, he's neither fish nor fowl.' He laughs: come on over. I buy a bottle of Camus before I arrive. His wife is at a training camp and his daughter is at their dacha. We drank, he started fucking me: he has a thick, curved dick and it won't fit into my mouth. He smears Vaseline all around my anus and whispers, 'I only come in asses, Olenka.' He slides in. I yell into the pillow, like I'd been cut, and he roars like a buffalo. He fucked a hole right into my guts and then we drank champagne. He says, 'Okay, I'll talk to the guys, but you have to apply to join the Komsomol immediately.' So that's what I did. And, a week later, they voted me onto the team. You already know what happened at the Olympics," she took her bathrobe from its hook.

"And Zhabin?"

"What about Zhabin?"

"Well . . . did you ever fuck again?"

"Of course. He fucked me all the time. As soon as he got the itch, he'd call me up at the dorm—brinng brinng: 'I'm waiting for you, blondie!' He always started in front and finished in the back."

"Did it hurt?"

"No. I got used to it. I even learned how to come from it . . . Oh!

What do we have here!" Olga noticed that Seryozha was covering his erect penis with his towel. "What bad manners you have!" she pulled his towel off and grabbed him by his cock. "Just what do you think you're doing, young man?"

Seryozha grabbed on to her.

"Can I try it in your butt, Ol?"

She smiled.

"Rebrov forbade us from corrupting you."

"Screw him! So . . . can I?"

"You want to that badly?"

"Mhmm."

She grabbed him by the ears, squeezed them. Looked into his eyes.

"You'll rat on me!"

"Never! That hurts, Ol . . ."

"You swear?"

"I swear! That hurts!"

"I'll take your word for it."

She walked out of the shower room and into the gym, got a tube of hand cream out of her gym bag, and beckoned to Seryozha with her finger. They walked over to a mat bundled up underneath a beam. Olga let her robe fall, squeezed cream into the palm of her hand, and, getting down onto her knees, began to rub it all over Seryozha's penis.

"The main thing is not to rush."

Then she rubbed the cream onto her anus and lay facedown on the mat. Seryozha got on top of her.

"Higher, higher," Olga spread her legs. "There. Do it harder. And don't rush . . ."

Seryozha began to move back and forth.

"My little boy . . . my little pussycat," Olga whispered, pressing her cheek against the mat. "Don't rush . . ."

Seryozha shuddered, moaned quietly, then froze.

"Already? My little pussycat . . ."

"He smears Vaseline all around my anus and whispers . . ."

"My little boy . . . my little pussycat," Olga whispered, pressing her cheek against the mat. "Don't rush . . ."

He rolled off of her, sat up, and touched his penis. Olga rolled over onto her back and stretched out.

"O-o-o-o-h! It's been a long time since Olga's been fucked in the brown place!"

"I'm thirsty," Seryozha stood up and walked over to the door.

"Bring me an orange!" Olga brought her legs up into the air, rolled backward, then sat up into the lotus position.

After lunch, Rebrov invited everyone into his office.

"I want to draw your attention to one very important circumstance," he began, sitting at his desk and looking down at his hands. "Operation No. 1 has been successfully completed, we have the rods and the intermediate block. Because of this, Operation No. 2 will not be carried out on the seventh of January, but on the thirty-first of December."

"But we've known this for a long time!" Shtaube shrugged.

"That's true. But you *don't* know something else." Rebrov opened a folder, pulled out a yellowed sheet of paper, and began to read it: "We must put an end to opportunistic complacency arising from the erroneous assumption that, as our forces grow, the enemy becomes tame and harmless, as if they were steroknepers. Such an assumption as to the root of the sterocone is incorrect. It is an eructation of the right deviation, assuring each and every individual that our enemies will slowly and quietly slide toward socialism, that, at the end of the day, they will become steroul with true socialists. It is not in the fashion of true Bolsheviks to rest steroshutsly on their laurels and lollygag around. We do not need complacency, but vigilance, a truly Bolshevik, revolutionary, and steropristosian vigilance. We must remember that the more hopeless the situation of our enemies becomes, the more desperately they will grab for some 'last resort,' as their only way forward, doomed as they are to a steromutunesh with Soviet power."

"What . . . is that?" asked Olga cautiously.

"From the appeal by the All-Union Communist Party of Bolsheviks to other party organizations on December second, 1934. It was corrected on the second, eighteenth, and twenty-first of December, 1980. There's more: 'December, Tuesday 22/4, the Great Martyr Anastasia of Sirmium (ca. 304). The martyrs Chrysogonus, Theodotus, Evodius, Evtikhian, and others (ca. 304). Hebrews 333. Zechariah 12: 25-26; 12: 22-25. Maccabees 43. Zecheriah: 10: 2-12.' Corrected on December 21, 1990."

Rebrov put the piece of paper back into the folder, sighed, and turned to the window.

After a prolonged silence, Shtaube hit his cane against the floor.

"Not everything depends on us, Viktor Valentinych! The stream cannot rise above its source. We do what we can, we try not to make mistakes. Everyone acts to the best of their abilities; Olenka and Seryozha and you and I. Everyone pushes until they sweat blood. I'm not talking about leniency, but about limits. About possibilities. Let me tell you, Viktor Valentinych . . ." the old man shook his head, "to demand the impossible from oneself and from others is as senseless as it is harmful. It will ruin the enterprise. When I set that greenhouse on fire, I poured gasoline over absolutely everything, I wasn't too lazy to shake out the file cabinet and dismantle Golubovsky's archive. I emptied all of the folders, splashed gas out of the canister, then, suddenly, I see a familiar photograph. I lifted it up and it was Rutman. Wearing a kosovorotka, a badge, and an axial. He's grinning like a zebra. The top corner of the back of the picture is marked 'July 4, 1957, Rylsk.' And in the middle, someone'd written: 'To our darling Svetozar. From Ilya, Seva, and Andrei on the day of the trial launch.' So there."

"That can't be."

"Oh it can, my darling. And next to the picture, I see a folder stuffed with documentation: reports, tables, and graphs."

"And you burned it?"

"Of course!"

Rebrov took out a cigarette and lit up.

"My deceased father used to say, 'Go ahead and dance on rooftops, but pay attention to the edge.' In our line of work, Henry Ivanych, there's no edge, just pits. And we must try to notice them in time. In order to do this, it is necessary to have a great many abilities. I read this document, not to frighten you, but for a specific purpose. The operation has been moved from the seventh of January to the thirty-first of December, not because of a gap in the allotment, but because of the znedo. And only because of the znedo."

"I think we already understood that a long time ago," Olga yawned. "I did at least."

"I did too!" Seryozha slapped his hands on his knees. "I remember everything about Denis. I give you my word as a Pioneer!"

"Don't brag before you know all the facts!" Shtaube waved his hand at him, stood up, his prosthesis creaking, and walked over to the window. "You know what, Viktor Valentinych, I read those books about Anna Akhmatova very carefully."

"The books I gave you?"

"Yes. Those ones . . ." Shtaube sighed, leaning onto his cane. "I read them and I understood that Anna Andreyevna Akhmatova does not suit us at all."

"Why?"

"Because . . ." Shtaube went silent and shook his head, then suddenly hit his cane against the floor, "because . . . that's just how it is, ladies and gentlemen! Who would do that?! What is that?! Why that beastliness once again?! That abomination?! With such people, I can't . . . I can't . . . Scum! Scum! And you add to it! They aren't humans! Bitch! Bitch! Beast! They . . . if you let them, they'll tear you up with their hooks."

"What . . . what do you mean?" Rebrov frowned uncomprehendingly.

"I'm not saying anything new! You have to be an orderly person and not a total bastard! I hate 'em! I'd hang 'em with no mercy! The way they trade! The way they shit on human values! I'd burn 'em alive, then feed 'em to the hogs! I'd shit upon their ugly mugs!"

"What are you babbling on about?"

"I'm not babbling! I've seen it all in my lifetime! I saw how they grabbed children by their legs and smashed 'em against birches! I saw how they hanged women! How they drove tractors over dead bodies! For me, my dear friends, understanding what it means to be respectable, to be . . . Yes! Yes! Respectable! For me, these aren't just empty words! I know what it means to have a pure and innocent soul!"

"You mean the thread?" Seryozha asked.

"Animals! Bastards! Filthy trash! I would smear 'em all over the walls! I would pour lead down their throats!"

"That's enough! Stop!" Rebrov smashed his hand against the table. "Explain to us exactly where you got this! How did you read the norp?"

"With my own eyes! These eyes here! 73, 18, 61, 22! Black and white!"

"78, 18, 61, 22," said Rebrov.

"What do you mean 78?! It's 73, not 78!"

"78, not 73. A typo."

"What do you mean a typo?"

"Well, they probably didn't smear the template properly and it printed the 8 as a 3."

"Fuck that! Are you sure that it's 78?"

"One hundred percent, Henry Ivanych."

"Puh, motherfucker!" Shtaube spat.

"Yes. 78, 18, 61, 22," Rebrov put his cigarette butt out in the ashtray. "Anna Andreyevna Akhmatova was a grand Russian poetess, an honest, deeply orderly woman who protected her pure and innocent soul through the terrible years of Bolshevism and, in what was a great national achievement, managed to glorify the Russian intelligentsia. Russia will never forget this. So there. But now let's discuss current affairs," he took the glass of water with the glans floating in it off of the shelf. "The showpiece has, so to speak, finished maturing: its edges are tattered, it's discolored, and so on. Olga Vladimirovna, go get a clean plate, cut the glans into thin strips, as you might cut up a mushroom, lay them out, and put them in the oven on low heat. The lowest heat. Open the door so that it doesn't cook, but dries out. As soon as it's totally dry, take this mortar and grind the glans into a powder. Then call me over. Everything clear?"

"Entirely," Olga nodded. "I have to change your bandages today, Henry Ivanych."

"I totally forgot!" Shtaube grinned. "Which means it doesn't hurt."

"One more thing. Do we have the meat grinder and the juicer?" Rebrov asked.

"We both checked them on the third day. Everything works."

"Will we have a Christmas tree?" Seryozha asked.

"You can deal with that. Grab the saw and go find a tree nearby. A small one, though."

"How big? As tall as me?"

"As tall as you and no taller," Rebrov put a pile of papers collated in a binder down in front of him. "The allotment will be tomorrow at twelve. The last one of the year. Please don't forget. You're free to go."

On December 31, shortly after 10:00 PM, Rebrov's car drove onto the territory of the dacha, stopped, and honked. The front door opened and Rebrov ran down the steps and along the cleared path leading to the car. He was wearing a dark-blue three-piece suit and carrying roses. Olga, Seryozha, and an elderly woman in an old-fashioned winter coat got out of the car.

"Vitenka!" she pronounced.

"Mom!" Rebrov walked over to her, hugged her, and began to kiss her. "Mother darling . . . at last . . . this is for you."

"My goodness! Summer roses . . . and I'm so late!"

"It's nothing, Mom. We got everything ready."

"The train was an hour late," Olga said, taking a bag out of the trunk, "Alexandra Olegovna and I almost missed each other."

"Yes, it's true!" the old woman laughed. "I somehow always end

"Anna Andreyevna Akhmatova was a grand Russian poetess . . . Go get a clean plate, cut the glans into thin strips, as you might cut up a mushroom, lay them out, and put them in the oven on low heat."

up on these little adventures! And thank God! Where's your coat, Vitya? You'll catch cold, darling."

"It's nothing, Mom. Let's go in, we've been ready to eat for a while."

They began walking toward the house.

"Ah, how glorious it is out here!" Alexandra Olegovna sighed. "A beautiful, quiet forest. After all of those trains . . . can you imagine, they didn't even serve tea!"

"The main thing is that you made it. How're you feeling?"

"Wonderfully, Vitenka, wonderfully. I'm so happy! You have such sweet friends! Olenka, Seryozha, and, ach, what a lovely house!"

She walked up the steps and into the entranceway.

"When was all of this built? Before the war?"

"In '49, Mom," Rebrov helped her take off her coat.

Shtaube came in wearing a tailcoat.

"Here, Mom, I'd like to introduce you to Henry Ivanovich Shtaube."

"Welcome, Alexandra Olegovna!" Shtaube kissed her hand.

"Thank you, Henry Ivanovich! It's very nice to meet you, Vitya wrote to me about you."

"And I've heard so much about you!" Shtaube smiled, holding her hand. "A day doesn't pass without Viktor Valentinovich talking about his mother!"

"He talked and talked about me, but not many letters from him do I see!" Alexandra Olegovna rhymed, shaking her finger at Rebrov. "Once a month and never more!"

"I repent, I repent," Rebrov bowed his head.

"Don't worry, Alexandra Olegovna, we'll reeducate him!" Shtaube offered her his twisted hand.

"I very much hope so!" the old woman took Shtaube by the hand.

They walked into the living room. There was a set table in the middle of the room and a Christmas tree covered in colorful lights by the window.

"Ach, how charming!" Alexandra Olegovna stopped. "Oh, how glorious it is here, my friends! I'm so happy, Vitya!"

"I'm happy too, Mom," Rebrov kissed her hand. "It's so nice that you're here."

"We were so worried about you that we got terribly hungry!" Shtaube smiled, walked over to the table, and lit the candles in the candelabra. "I hope that you are too?"

"How could I not be! Looking at a table like this! It's wonderful! But, but, but!" she raised her finger. "You happen to be missing just the thing I've brought! Can you guess what it is, Vitya?"

"Sturgeon caviar? Balyk?"

She shook her head.

"No one even *remembers* when they could get delicacies like that in Saratov. Give me my bag, please."

"Here you go, Mom."

Alexandra Olegovna removed a jar from her bag, took off the lid, and handed it to Rebrov.

"Crayfish tails!" Rebrov exclaimed. "Crayfish tails in a wine sauce! Incredible! Do you remember what I told you, Henry Ivanych? Olga Vladimirovna! Seryozha! Where are they?"

"They're changing," Shtaube took the jar from Rebrov and sniffed at it. "That smell could drive you insane!"

"It was my deceased husband, Vitya's father, Valentine Evgrafovich's favorite chaser. There was a time when they sold crayfish on every corner in Saratov: like sunflower seeds. Now it's a delicacy, just like caviar!"

"This is unbelievable, Mom! The taste of my childhood. Out on the terrace, sunset, Dad's there, Anatoly Ivanovich, Zoya Borisovna . . . Misha. Is he still alive?"

"Mikhail Matveyich? Of course! He was just assigned a new apartment by the bridge. Ninochka got married and he'll be a great-grandpa soon. He sends his warm wishes."

"Thanks."

Olga and Seryozha came in. Olga was wearing a long evening dress made of dark-purple velvet and Seryozha was dressed in a white silk shirt with a huge golden-black bowtie, black, gold-threaded breeches, white, knee-high socks, and black patent-leather shoes studded with silver stars.

"Ach, how charming!" Alexandra Olegovna clasped her hands together. "What a wife you have, Vitya! You're stunningly beautiful, Olenka, and you look so similar to Greta Garbo! Except you're more beautiful, more graceful, and more feminine! And Seryozha! The young prince! The heir to the throne!"

"What about me?" Shtaube merrily assumed a dignified air.

"You're a baron, the ruler of a marvelous castle near Moscow!"

"Is that all?" Shtaube raised his eyebrows.

Everyone laughed.

"To the table, ladies and gentlemen," Rebrov clapped.

"To the table!" Seryozha jumped up and did a little pirouette.

"With great pleasure!" Alexandra Olegovna smiled.

They sat down at the table. Rebrov poured wine for the women, vodka for himself and Shtaube, and orange juice for Seryozha.

"My friends . . ." Rebrov began, but Shtaube raised his glass.

"No, no, Viktor Valentinych. In accordance with my rights as host, I ask to be the first to speak."

"Let him, Vitya!" Alexandra Olegovna advised.

Rebrov bowed his head.

"My friends," began Shtaube, "this is a truly special evening: this merit pensioner, you see, this Minister of Secondary Mechanical Engineering from the Glorious Era of Stagnation, has found himself under the weight of a whole ton of happiness. For an old man like me, comrades, this is too much!"

Everyone laughed.

"It's true, judge for yourselves: without all of you, I'd be sitting at home on Kutuzovsky Avenue with my housekeeper, one Maria Mikhailovna, we'd watch TV and share a quiet meal. At twelve, we'd drink a little champagne (warm champagne, so that I wouldn't get a sore throat), and by one, I'd already be the Mayor of Snoreville . . ."

"Excuse me, Henry Ivanych, but what about your old colleagues? What about childhood friends?"

"A-a-a well, as Pushkin once wrote, some are gone and some are far away. You know, Alexandra Olegovna, I only had three true friends in my youth: one died in the war, one died at Beria's while being interrogated, and one died two years ago from a heart attack. This isn't what I want to talk about though. I want to talk about the fact that holy places are never empty. And now, I will move to the main section of my speech. Thank you for bringing your son into the world, Alexandra Olegovna. Thank you from me and from the entire Ministry of Secondary Mechanical Engineering. I've never had the honor of working with a more orderly, honest, and professional member of a younger generation. And I'll tell you something in all sincerity: if Gorbachev and his cronies hadn't made me retire four years ago, Viktor would certainly be my second-in-command. Without a doubt! But I'm also sure that he'll manage to reach the top without me. He has everything he needs to do so . . ."

"Henry Ivanych," Rebrov shook his head. "Why are you talking so much about me . . ."

"You be quiet. We're not talking about you."

"If you say so!"

Everyone laughed.

"Comrades, we are talking about the wonderful Alexandra Olegovna Rebrova, who has come to visit us from Saratov on the occasion of the New Year! No one has given us a gift like this in a long time! And so, I'd like to dedicate my first toast to the health of Alexandra Olegovna!"

"Hooray!" Seryozha shouted.

Everyone clinked glasses with Alexandra Olegovna and drank.

"Ah, what wonderful wine!" the old woman carefully put her half-empty glass back on the table. "But I think the food that goes with it will be even better!"

"Please, my friends!" Shtaube tucked his napkin into his collar. "We're all terribly hungry!"

They ate in silence for a little while.

"Is it true that you ran across the Volga once when it was frozen, Alexandra Olegovna?" Seryozha asked.

"It was the Ural, Seryozhenka," the old woman smiled.

"And were there cracks?"

"There were. And the ice was trembling beneath me. I ran across the river and, the next day, the ice flowed away!"

"When was that?" Olga asked.

"In '44. We'd celebrated my birthday the day before and were up late. So, I overslept by an hour and a half and missed my bus, which took us from one side of the Ural to another over a bridge. In those days, Seryozha, there was a twenty-minute rule for all enterprises: if a person was more than twenty minutes late to work, they were arrested and sent to trial. I took the quickest path I could because I really didn't want to have served a second sentence at twenty-six."

"Twenty-six? I'm twenty-six!" Olga said. "What was your enterprise?"

"A hospital."

"And what was your first sentence for?" Seryozha asked.

"My friends!" Shtaube raised his glass. "There's someone among us who's lived an incredible life. If you'd like for Alexandra Olegovna to run through her biography for us, then I ask you to raise your glass!"

"Oh goodness, an autobiography!" the old woman laughed, clinking glasses with everyone. "Really, I'm not ready!"

"Please, please!"

"Please!"

"Tell us, Mom!"

"Well . . . let me take a drink first! For courage!"

They all drank.

"Well, my darlings," Alexandra Olegovna wiped her lips with a napkin, "to put it mildly, the path my life has taken has never been a simple one. Zigzag after zigzag. I was born in 1918 in Moscow to one Oleg Borisovich Rebrov, a colonel in the Imperial Russian Army. I only know my father from pictures and from the stories my mother and older brother would tell. The Bolsheviks shot him when I was three months old. My mother, Lydia Nikolaevna Gorskaya, was the daughter of a well-known ophthalmologist, Professor Nikolai Valerianovich Gorsky, thanks to whom our family was able to survive the years of war communism. He treated Sverdlov, Trotsky, Kalinin, and Krupskaya. Helped them to better see the class enemy. They gave us food because of that and even allowed us to stay in our house on Povarskaya, a street later renamed for some bandit named Vorovsky. Good his name lets us know he's a *vor*—a thief—an *accurate* name. Then Grandpa died in 1925 and they immediately kicked us out of our house. My brother Alyosha fled to Paris through Poland. We were given shelter by my father's former colleague who'd become a high-ranking military specialist for the Bolsheviks. He soon proposed to my mother and they were married. As far as I can remember, Mother didn't love Ivan Ivanovich, though he loved her very much and treated me with great tenderness. Everything was good until '38: I got into medical school and made it through the first three years, Mother did translations, and my stepfather served in the general's staff. On the third of May, I came home from school and found NKVD agents digging through our things. All of our books were splayed out on the floor and these men were walking on them like they were a carpet. They told me that my stepfather had been arrested. I asked: where's my mother? They said that she'd become overexcited during Ivan Ivanovich's arrest, then had fallen ill, and they'd had to call an ambulance, which had taken her away. In fact, one of those NKVD bastards had found a medallion with my father's hair in it and shaken the hairs out. And told my mother: 'you hang on to all sorts of junk.' She'd slapped him, for which he'd hit her in the temple with the butt of his revolver. When I got to Sklifosovsky Hospital, Mother was already at death's door and was falling in and out of consciousness. Her temple was fractured and she was taken in for an operation, but died on the table. 'A loss of consciousness, which caused a fall and trauma to the skull.' That's what was written in the autopsy report. There you have it, my darlings. They buried my mother. Kicked me out of school. Immediately after the funeral, the building manager came with a precinct police officer, showing me an order about 'densification of the living space.' A stoker's family came to live with me. My friends insisted that I leave Moscow. I didn't listen. They came for me on the sixth of June. Lubyanka. They tortured me for a month. I didn't sign anything. Article 58, Line 11. Ten years. We traveled to Kotlas on the Stolypin. We were transferred. They immediately took us to the baths and, in the dressing room, there was a wide, old mirror on the wall. Everyone ran to the mirror. I did too. And then I see: a horde of naked women, emaciated faces, everyone jostling around, and I can't find myself, I really can't! And suddenly I saw my mother. She was looking at me from inside the mirror. I ran my hand across my face and so did she. I touched my hair and so did she. Ever since that day, I try not to look in the mirror. Then—the camp. At first it was terribly difficult; the shared labor was just killing me. And suddenly, in the cafeteria, a friend of my father's comes up to me: Sergei Apollinarievich Boldin, a former regimental doctor. He arranged to have me work as a nurse in the infirmary, saving me from certain death. After three or so years of that, I had an incredible spot of luck: they reopened my case and let me free for 'the lack of the element of a crime'! About twenty other people were also set free from the camp. This was after Yezhov was shot and Beria came to power. We went to Moscow and prayed for Beria's health. Even so, I wasn't allowed to register in Moscow and had nowhere to live and, more importantly, nothing to live on. I went to Guryev, to Aunt Veronica. She worked as a surgeon in a hospital and she took me on as her assistant. That's how I came to live in dusty Guryev during the whole war. I talked to exiled intellectuals, to Cossacks, to Kazakhs . . . There was a lot of fish there, but not much flour. I ate spoonfuls of caviar, dreaming about bread. I also ate camel meat."

"Was it tasty?" Seryozha asked.

"I can't remember. Back then, I didn't care. The war ended and Aunt Veronica's son Valentine came back from the front. We immediately fell in love and got married not long after. Our happy family didn't last for very long: on November ninth, 1948, they arrested me again. Then they arrested Valentine. I was in the sixth month of my pregnancy and, this time, I didn't hold up as well: I signed everything. All of their fantasies. All in all, the second time was harder than the first. Much harder. I was afraid for my child, but this turned out to be unnecessary: it was a stillbirth. The camp was in Mordovia. But fortune smiled on me once again: I got a position in the sewing workshop. Mhmm. They write a lot about the camps these days. Many of these publications are very truthful, but, I'll tell you, it's impossible to imagine life in the camps. That's why I don't like talking about it. Not because it's painful or uncomfortable, no! It's just pointless. They let me go in the fall of 1954. I went back to Guryev. Slept for days. Then I got ready to go to Igarka— to Valentine's camp. My aunt went to the market and brought me balyk, sturgeon caviar, honey, nuts, and baked rolls. And we're sitting there one evening, putting everything into a knapsack when suddenly—a knock at the door. My aunt went to open it and didn't come back. I called her and she didn't reply. I stand up and start to walk over. And then I see—she and Valentine are standing there just hugging each other. It turns out that they let us both free on the same day . . ." Alexandra Olegovna wiped away her tears, sighed, and cheerfully finished her story: "and one year later, I gave birth to this young man!"

"Yes!" Shtaube shook his head. "Now I understand why Viktor is so single-minded."

"You didn't know Vitya's father, Henry Ivanovich!" Alexandra Olegovna shook her finger at him. "Don't make hasty conclusions!"

Everyone laughed.

"Let's drink to the entire Rebrov family!" Olga lifted her glass. "You are all true heroes. While I was listening . . . I . . . just didn't know what to say. You're a hero, Alexandra Olegovna. May God give you health and happiness."

"Thank you darling," the old woman took a drink of wine. "But, actually, there are millions of such stories in Russia. Things didn't turn out nearly as badly as they could have for me."

"Many people's lives were ruined when they were illegally repressed," Shtaube sighed, "but if we're talking about the NKVD, I have to say that it wasn't just scumbags working there. There were some honest people too."

"I never met any," Alexandra Olegovna said quietly.

"It's already fifteen minutes to twelve!" Seryozha cried out, looking at the clock.

"Champagne! Where's the champagne?"

"We have to turn on the TV!"

"It came so quick!"

"Calm down, my friends, no need to panic!" Rebrov stood up and walked over to Alexandra Olegovna. "We have a gift for you, Mom, a gift that you need to receive before 1990 flies away."

"What kind of gift is it?"

"A very serious one, Alexandra Olegovna!" Olga stood up. "You need it before the year is up!"

"That's enough fuss!" Rebrov stood behind the old lady. "Close your eyes, Mom."

The old woman closed her eyes. Olga took her by the left arm and Shtaube by the right. Rebrov took a noose out of his pocket and put it around Alexandra Olegovna's neck.

"Be careful! That tickles!" she laughed.

"Hup," commanded Rebrov and sharply tightened the noose.

Alexandra Olegovna began to wiggle anxiously and wheeze.

"The arms, the arms!" Rebrov muttered.

Olga and Shtaube kept tight hold of the old woman. Her head trembled gently and her left leg began to beat against the leg of a chair. The dishes rang out and one glass tumbled over.

"Keep holding her tight!" Rebrov whispered.

The beat of Alexandra Olegovna's leg began to weaken and she passed gas. A shudder came over her body and she went limp. Several minutes later, Rebrov loosened the noose.

"18 and 6," Seryozha smiled. "There are paper lumps on the bears. And a roll."

"The old bag farted . . ." Shtaube frowned.

Rebrov removed the noose. They lay the corpse out on the floor.

"So. A moment of your attention," Rebrov straightened up. "First of all, everyone needs to change. Second of all, you need to remember the division of labor and not interfere with each other's work. And the third thing, ladies and gentlemen. Today, our entire operation depends on your exactitude, professionalism, and calmness. Try to remember this. As long as everything goes according to plan and we stay on the right path, fortune will smile upon us. We don't have the right to screw up. Let's move."

They changed into their white robes, put on rubber gloves, dragged the corpse into a spacious bathroom, and locked the door. Here, everything was already laid out: the instruments, the dishes, and the appliances. They undressed the corpse. Alexandra Olegovna's long blue drawers were stained with fresh fecal matter.

"I guess she didn't just fart?" Seryozha smiled.

Rebrov and Olga bound the corpse's legs and, with Shtaube's help, hung it upside down on a hook fixed into the ceiling above the bath. Seryozha put a ten-liter pail into the bath. Rebrov turned on the electric saw, cut off the head and put it into a plastic bag Olga was holding. Blood flowed from the neck and into the pail.

"Olga Vladimirovna, Seryozha," Rebrov muttered, moving the pail into a more advantageous position, "burn her clothes and personal effects in the fireplace. Put her papers on the table. I'll be waiting for you here in a half hour."

Having gathered the clothing, Olga and Seryozha left.

"So. The head," Rebrov turned to Shtaube. Shtaube handed him the bag. Rebrov took out the head and put it on an enamel plate, turned on the electric saw, and cut the head in two. Shtaube took half of the head, put it into a press frame, and pushed a red button. The press started to work, slowly squeezing the half head. Shtaube placed a three-liter pail under the chute. Pressed liquid flowed into the pail. Rebrov filtered the pomace into a bucket. A half hour later, Olga and Seryozha came in. Almost all of the corpse's blood had run into the pail. Rebrov took the electric saw and cut off a piece of one of the buttocks and gave it to Olga, who immediately put it into the meat grinder, which ground the meat into mince, which fell into the intake of the juice press, which turned the mince into juice, which flowed into the ten-liter pail. Rebrov cut off another piece and handed it to Olga. Seryozha was responsible for the meat grinder and Shtaube was responsible for the juicer. In less than three hours, the corpse's meat and insides had been processed. Rebrov sawed the skeleton into tiny pieces, which Olga and Shtaube also put into the juice press. When the process had been completed, the blood and juice were transferred to a thirty-liter tank and moved into the living room. They then thoroughly cleaned the bathtub, dishes, appliances, and instruments. They dumped the pomace in the garden and covered it over with snow. Then everyone changed clothes and gathered together in the living room. Rebrov walked over to the tank and removed the lid.

"Twenty-eight liters. You turned out to be right, Henry Ivanych."

"I have a trained eye," Shtaube laughed, sitting down at the table and pouring himself some vodka.

"Oy, I'm so tired," Olga lay down on the carpet next to the tank. "It's already four? Let's at least have a little champagne."

"First we must *pour*. Only then can we drink. Seryozha! Bring us the suitcase."

Rebrov took a noose out of his pocket and put it around Alexandra Olegovna's neck.

Almost all of the corpse's blood had run into the pail.

Seryozha brought in a brown suitcase with metal corners and put it next to the tank. Rebrov used a little key to undo a lock on the left side of the suitcase and carefully removed it: the lock turned out to be a giant rubber stopper. Seryozha inserted a wide funnel into the hole. Rebrov and Shtaube lifted the tank and poured its contents into the suitcase.

"There we go," Rebrov put the stopper back in place and locked it, "now we can have some champagne . . ."

Shtaube uncorked a bottle and filled four glasses.

"This is the first time in my life I haven't celebrated the New Year," Olga took a glass and looked through the liquid at the candles.

"Same here!" Seryozha took a drink from his glass.

"Congratulations, my friends," Rebrov smiled exhaustedly, "now we have the liquid mother."

"Happy New Year."

"Hooray!"

They clinked glasses and drank.

"Who wants mutton?" asked Olga.

Seryozha and Shtaube raised their hands.

"If you don't mind, I'm going to bed," Rebrov rubbed his temples.

"Yes, Vitya. You're very pale. You look tired."

"Did you get overexcited, maybe?"

"Yes . . . everything that's happened . . . my heart's all tingly," he took a mandarin, looked at it, then put it back. "Take the liquid mother into the smaller cellar. Good night, everyone."

He left.

"Let's go by the fireplace, guys," Olga suggested, "it's too cold here. We'll warm the mutton over the fire and cuddle up on the furs."

"Not a bad idea," Shtaube drank some champagne, "first I'll take the liquid mother downstairs."

"You'll manage alone?"

"I could carry you to the guard post and back, my darling!" Shtaube exclaimed defensively.

"Really now?" Olga smiled.

•

Shtaube threw a bone on the fire, licked his fingers, and reached for the bottle of vodka.

"One more, Olenka."

"No objections here," Olga was lying on the bearskin rug and eating a pear. Seryozha was sleeping on the sofa, wrapped in a blanket.

"You have to understand these people too," Shtaube handed Olga a glass. "Imagine, they earned an honest living, they exceeded their normal quotas, lived in a constant state of hunger, defended their Motherland, and then they're told: you're a joke, your life was just a big mistake, you weren't building a glorious future, but a shitty lil' concentration camp run by fucking Stalin called the Union of Soviet Socialist Republics! And for that, you motherfuckers, your children and grandchildren warmly congratulate you!"

He belched, took a drink, and wiped his lips with a blanket.

"I dunno," Olga took a drink and then bit into her pear. "Inka Besyayeva told me about how she and her girlfriends were taken to a Central Committee dacha and how *that* ended."

"How?"

"With a corpse. The senior coach of the Spartakiad took his lover Innochka and two of her girlfriends to this house. It turned out that the head of the Central Committee was there too. And also Deputy Tyazhelnikova and some dickhead from the Central Committee of the Komsomol. They drank, had a bite to eat, and then went to the bath-house. They started to fuck. And this girl choked on the Komsomol guy's sperm. She choked to death. And then . . ."

"A sreez of the forp to the Yashchenkovians! There are party appa-ratchiks, but there are also true communists, it's not that fucking compli-cated! Yeltsin, for example, was a true communist!"

"I don't like Yeltsin. He has such a heavy face . . ."

"The main thing is that a person does his job. For an honest communist, this means thinking about the needs of the people, help-ing to facilitate production, and taking care of the poor. But, for party apparatchiks, the main thing is career goals, the chain of command, and brown-nosing! Pussies like that are ready to crawl into their bosses' asses like worms and come out of their mouths! We should crush 'em like nits! An honest communist is a bother to no one. Even private owners."

"My dad was an honest communist," Olga smoothed the outside of her cigarette and lit up, "so he was always fighting with the party bosses. He got two official demerits and had two heart attacks."

"Or they say: Stalin, Stalin! A villain and a murderer. They seem to have forgotten that he turned an agrarian country into an industrial one. It's true that the cult of personality is very fuckin' unnecessary. But these fucks need discipline like an unbroken horse needs a collar! Without dis-cipline, look what we get up to: killing, burning, and racketeering! If Stalin were still here, he'd show 'em what it means to racketeer! He'd set up such a racket that everyone would piss and shit nonstop! They'd racketeer timber right up the river in Siberia!"

"My dad also respected Stalin, but not for his industrial reforms: for the Great War . . ."

"For the war?! For that, he should be boiled alive and thrown to the dogs! The pockmarked piece of shit beheaded the army, shot Tukhachevsky and Yakir, and put honest commanders in jail! He pro-moted cocksuckers like Mekhlis! He let the Germans bomb our whole air force to shit on the very first day!"

Olga shuddered and her cigarette fell from her fingers. She put her hands over her face and sobbed.

"What? What is it?" Shtaube knelt down to her.

"I don't want to . . . don't want . . . the zhuok . . ." she moaned.

"Forget about it . . ." he laid his hand on her shoulder, "are you afraid?"

"I'm not afraid! I just don't want it to be Nina!"

Shtaube sighed, picked up her cigarette, and threw it into the fire.

"Olga Vladimirovna, Nina is well prepared. No worse than Sokolov, right?"

"I don't want to . . . I don't want to!" Olga sobbed.

"The zhuok's been around for a while, why're you torturing yourself? Better to have a drink and chase away this sad melancholy. We all need our anesthesia."

He poured the rest of the vodka into their glasses, put the mouth of the bottle to his lips, and blew on it. The bottle produced a prolonged sound.

The week passed in preparation for Operation No. 3. On the eighth of January at 9:12, everyone was gathered together in Rebrov's office.

"I'd like for everyone to change the time on their watches," Rebrov said, "it is now 11:28."

He waited while Shtaube, Olga, and Seryozha moved the hands on their watches, then continued.

"And so, Operation No. 3. Our future depends on its outcome. We do not have the right to stumble. Nor do we have the right to cowardice, indecision, or a lack of professionalism. At 12:10, we will enter the ministry. At 12:30, we should be leaving with a ready result. At 12:45—the factory. After that, the schedule depends on circumstance. Are there any questions?"

"Can I carry it?" Seryozha asked.

"No," Rebrov stood up. "Okay, let's move."

"Go with God," Shtaube mumbled.

They went downstairs, put their outer layers on, and left the house.

"It melted a little again," Olga squinted at the dim sun.

"I wanna roll a fatty," Seryozha said.

"There'll be time to roll fatties . . . later . . ." Rebrov pronounced distractedly.

They got into the car and set off. At 12:02, Rebrov turned off of the Garden Ring and onto Malaya Bronnaya, drove into the courtyard of building number 8, and turned off the engine.

"You'll be third, Henry Ivanych," Rebrov said, taking the attaché case from Shtaube.

"I remember perfectly well," Shtaube said frustratedly.

"You better not get in the way!" Olga slapped Seryozha's hat. "Take deep breaths and follow Mommy. I'll kill you if not!"

They got out of the car, started to walk along Zholtovsky Street, turned right, and found themselves in front of the Ministry of Special Works. Rebrov walked up to the massive door, turned the handle, and walked in. He was dressed in a gray sheepskin coat, a deerskin hat, and a light-grey mohair scarf; he was carrying the black attaché case in his left hand. Olga came in behind him wearing a long, blue, puffy jacket and an oblong handbag. Shtaube came in after her, leaning on his cane, wearing the winter uniform of a colonel of the Military Engineers, and carrying a brown briefcase. Seryozha followed after them wearing his normal clothes. They walked through the vestibule and found themselves in a large lobby with marble columns. On the right, a guard was sitting in a glass-windowed office and a policeman was wandering around in front of the wide main staircase. There were only a few other people in the lobby.

"Hey now, why are you so shy?" Shtaube turned to Seryozha. "You always ask about the ministry, right? Well, here it is: Grandpa's famous ministry!"

They approached the guard.

"Here to see Zlotnikov," Rebrov gave the guard his and Olga's passports. The guard wrote out two passes.

"We're here to see Nikolai Nikolaevich Artamonov, my old friend!" Shtaube handed him his passport. "After I retired ten years ago, everything in the ministry changed! Even the guard post. It was made of wood and now it's made of glass!"

The guard smiled.

"The boy's with you?"

"The lil' cadet's with me!"

The guard wrote out a pass and handed back Shtaube's passport.

Without hurrying, all four of them deposited their coats in the cloak-room and walked past the policeman and toward the elevators. When they got inside, Rebrov pressed the button for 2.

"When I say 'hup,' Olga Vladimirovna."

They got off on the second floor and walked down the wide, oak-pan-eled hallway, which ended in a large atrium. A red carpet led all the way down the hallway to the main door:

Minister of Special Works
RADCHENKO
Valery Pavlovich

There were five more doors in the atrium:

First Deputy Minister
MAZDIN Yuri Prokofievich
Deputy Minister
SMIRNOV Nikolai Igorevich
Deputy Minister
SHUSHANIA Georgy Avtandilovich
Deputy Minister
NIKULIN Viktor Nikolaevich
Deputy Minister
BODRYAGIN Mikhail Mikhailovich

Rebrov walked over to the door of Nikulin's office, opened it, and was the first to enter. There was a secretary in the waiting room.

"Hello," Rebrov pronounced loudly.

"Hello," the secretary replied.

Shtaube, Olga, and Seryozha also walked in.

"Is Viktor Nikolaevich in?"

"Do you have an appointment?" the secretary looked at them.

Shtaube smiled.

"Old friends don't need appointments, darling. They're invited to come visit."

"I understand," she said, picking up the phone. "Who shall I say is here?"

"Say 'hup' is here," said Rebrov stepping off to the side. Olga pulled her pistol with its silencer out of her bag and shot the secretary twice in the head. The secretary fell back into her chair. Rebrov took the phone out of her hand, put it back into its cradle, opened the middle drawer of her desk, found keys, and threw them to Shtaube. Shtaube locked the door out to the hallway with the keys. Rebrov walked into the office of the assistant deputy minister. He was in his office with a typist.

"Hello, comrades. Hup," said Rebrov and stepped off to the side. Olga immediately shot both of them in the head. The assistant deputy minister grabbed his face with his hands, stood up, then fell to the floor. The typist slid down from her chair with a moan. Olga ran up to them and fired again. Rebrov walked into the waiting room.

"Vigilance and tension."

Shtaube opened the door of the main office, letting Rebrov go in first. Rebrov walked in. Nikulin was sitting at his desk and dictating something to a stenographer sitting opposite him.

"Hello, Viktor Nikolaevich. Hup to her," Rebrov pronounced loudly. Olga shot the stenographer in the head twice. The stenographer screamed and fell to the ground. Nikulin stared at the stenographer.

"Viktor Nikolaevich, call Kolosov and tell him that Yakushev the driver needs to come up to the minister's waiting room now," Rebrov said.

Nikulin was still staring at the stenographer. Blood was flowing from her busted head and onto the table.

"Did you understand what I just said?"

Nikulin looked at Rebrov. Olga pointed the pistol at him.

"Call, motherfucker!" Rebrov spoke through clenched teeth. "We're not gonna wait!"

Nikulin picked up the phone and pressed a bottom on the intercom.

"Boris . . . Boris Ilyich. Yes. Here . . . this . . . Find Yakushev . . . the driver . . . get him to come up to Valery Palych. Yes. It's urgent. Yes."

He put down the phone.

"Now, a moment of your attention," Rebrov looked scornfully into Nikulin's eyes, "you're going to go to Radchenko with us and help with one simple matter. It won't take more than fifteen minutes. Your life depends entirely on a successful outcome. Attaining this successful outcome won't demand much from you, Viktor Nikolaevich: total obedience, responsiveness to the situation, and a dash of inwardly directed tension. You understand?"

Nikulin looked at him.

"You understand?" Rebrov repeated. Olga put the barrel of the gun to Nikulin's forehead.

"That . . . won't be necessary," Nikulin pulled away. "I understand."

"Let's move," Rebrov straightened up.

Nikulin got up from the desk and walked over to the door.

"You first. Act natural."

Olga replaced the clip and put the gun into her purse.

They walked out into the atrium. Shtaube locked the door and gave the keys to Seryozha. Two people came out of Smirnov's office, talking as they walked through the atrium. Nikulin walked into the minister's waiting room. Rebrov, Shtaube, Olga, and Seryozha walked in behind him. An assistant minister, a secretary, and a visitor were all sitting in the waiting room.

"Hullo," Nikulin said languidly.

"Hup," Rebrov pushed Nikulin off to the side. Olga shot all three of them in the head. Shtaube locked the door out to the atrium. Rebrov nodded at the door with a plaque on it that read: DESK OFFICER. Nikulin stepped over the visitor's legs and approached the door.

"Stop. How many people are in there?"

"Five . . . no . . . seven," Nikulin looked at the plaque.

"Open the door and ask three of them to come out here."

Nikulin grabbed the door handle, turned it, and cracked the door.

"Pyotr . . . Sergeyich, can I ask you for . . . a minute . . . and the translators too . . ."

"You get out of the way," Olga mumbled, standing behind the door. Nikulin walked over to the assistant deputy minister's desk. Olga managed to hit the desk officer in the temple right when he walked through the door, then shot the translators in the head as they came out behind the desk officer. Pushing past their falling bodies, she ran into the desk officer's office and opened fire on the four colleagues remaining. One of them managed to cry out. Olga replaced the clip, finished off the twitching typist, and left the room.

"Forward!" Rebrov nodded to Nikulin.

Nikulin walked into the minister's office, which was separated from the waiting room by two massive oaken doors. Olga, Rebrov, and Shtaube came in behind Nikulin. Radchenko was talking on the phone and sitting behind an enormous desk made of red wood.

"What's the deal?" he asked, covering the phone with his palm. "Why weren't you announced?"

"Valery . . . Pavlovich . . . it's . . ." Nikulin pronounced palely, then fell to his knees. He vomited on the carpet. Olga shot one of the minister's six phones three times.

"What? What? What?" dropping the phone, Radchenko started to get up from his leather chair.

"Calm down, Valery Pavlovich," Rebrov said, nodding to Shtaube, "Comrade Colonel will explain everything."

Leaving his briefcase on the carpet, Shtaube walked over to Radchenko, took a brass knuckle with two rows of steel studs out of his pocket, and punched the minister in the face. Radchenko fell back into the armchair, putting his hands over his face.

"Where are the fundaments?" Shtaube rested his cane against the desk and sat down on its edge. "Orel or Krasnoyarsk?"

"Terekhov," Nikulin mumbled, wiping his mouth.

"Hup," Rebrov nodded toward Nikulin. Olga shot him in the back of the head.

"Orel or Krasnoyarsk?" Shtaube brought his face to Radchenko's drooling mouth and punched his hands, which were still clutched over his eyes.

"Orel . . . Orel . . ." Radchenko moaned.

Seryozha ran in from the waiting room.

"They're knocking!"

"It's Yakushev!" Rebrov and Olga ran out and came back with Yakushev and Leontiev. Yakushev angrily pushed Leontiev and Leontiev fell down, rose back up, and began to get undressed with trembling hands.

"Is the map in the special safe?" Shtaube asked.

Radchenko nodded weakly. The telephone rang.

"Back in November, this piece of shit . . . this bastard!" Yakoshev spat on Leontiev.

"How many kilometers is it from Krasnoyarsk?" Shtaube put the brass knuckles back into his pocket and got down from the desk.

"Seventy . . ." Radchenko pronounced.

"In which direction?"

"West . . . western . . ."

"Any landmarks?"

"I've . . . never been there . . . I can't remember without a map . . ." Radchenko sobbed, "just please don't . . . kill me."

"Well, is there anything nearby!?" Rebrov opened his attaché case. "A river? A village?"

"It's right on the Chulym! After you pass Achinsk and the Kozulka Station," Leontiev, now naked, mumbled quickly, "and then you turn right and, hmm, a kilometer as the bird flies later the Chulym begins and you follow the Chulym for a little while along the hills . . ."

"What about Terekhov?" Rebrov took an electric knife out of the attaché case and started to look around for a plug.

"Terekhov . . ." Leontiev shrugged and licked his dry lips. Radchenko, still crying, uncovered his bloody face.

"Terekh . . . ov . . . Terekhov is already . . . already . . ."

Rebrov and Shtaube exchanged a look.

"Ah, motherfucker!" Shtaube clapped joyfully.

"Hup," Rebrov commanded, sticking the plug into the socket. Olga shot Leontiev in the head and he fell down onto the carpet. Rebrov and Shtaube turned him over onto his back and Rebrov began to cut into his chest with the electric knife.

"When they told me . . . I didn't believe . . ." Radchenko sobbed, wiping his face with his sleeve, "I was sure . . . that it was just a provocation. A cunning . . . provocation . . ."

"What's the time?" Rebrov put a piece of Leontiev's chest into the plastic bag Shtaube was holding out to him.

"Thirty," Olga looked at her watch.

"Quick!" Rebrov put the bag into the attaché case, Shtaube pulled a folder of documents out of his briefcase, opened it in front of Radchenko, and held out a pen.

"Come on."

Radchenko signed.

"Stop dripping, asshole," Shtaube shoved Radchenko's head to the side and dabbed at two drops of blood that'd fallen onto the document with a paperweight.

"Quick, quick!" Rebrov was waiting with his hand out. Shtaube handed him the folder and Rebrov put it into the attaché case.

"Hup, hup."

Olga shot Radchenko in the head.

"Main exit?" Yakushev asked.

"No chance," Rebrov answered as he walked.

They walked into the minister's break room, opened the door, and walked down the stairs into the inner courtyard of the ministry. There were about twenty cars there. They got into a black ZIL-110 and Yakushev started the engine.

"You get everything shifted alright?" Rebrov asked.

"Right after you did," Yakushev started the car, drove up to the gates, and honked. The gates began to open slowly.

"We're running out of time!" Rebrov twitched.

"We're right on time," Shtaube spat onto his bloodstained hand and began to rub at it with a handkerchief. They turned onto Malaya Bronnaya, then onto the Garden Ring, reached Mayakovsky Square, and turned onto Gorky Street.

"Give me your segment, Henry Ivanych," Rebrov asked without turning around.

Shtaube took the segment out of his jacket pocket and handed it to Rebrov. Rebrov applied his segment to Shtaube's segment, pressed them together, and connected the locks. The red scales coincided at 8.3 and the black scales at 8.7. Rebrov looked at his watch, did a calculation on his pocket calculator, and moved the teeth of the segments.

"27, 10, 6."

"Well thank God!" Shtaube took back his segment. "You always want it to be so perfectly . . . ideal!"

"Oh, it'll be perfectly ideal . . . when pigs fly!!" Rebrov sighed irritably.

"Don't tempt fate, Viktor Valentinych!"

"Will you need the support there, Vitya?" having unbuttoned her jacket, Olga stuffed new clips into the cartridge belt.

"No."

"Be careful with Sergeyev," Yakushev said. "He could've sniffed around with Leontiev in Urengoy. Pavlov too."

"Should I do the shet?" Seryozha twisted his Rubik's cube.

"Yes, yes. But keep it simple."

At 12:49, they drove up to the main gates of the Borets factory. Yakushev honked. A guard looked in through the window, then disappeared. The gates opened.

"If Shagin's weaseled his way out of this, then you'll lead," Rebrov said to Yakushev.

"What about the ZIL?"

"I got it."

The car drove onto the territory of the factory and stopped in front of the foundry. They didn't have time to get out of the car before Sergeyev, Barmin, and Khlebnikov walked over to them.

"Hello, comrades!" Sergeyev pronounced cheerfully.

"Hullo," Rebrov nodded drily and, without shaking their hands, walked over to the entrance.

"What is this . . . why are you dressed so lightly?" Sergeyev smiled awkwardly and helped Shtaube to get out of the car. "You'll catch cold in no time . . ."

"It's nothing, we'll warm up in a sec . . ." without even looking at Sergeyev, Shtaube limped after Rebrov.

Olga put her hands on Seryozha's shoulders and they passed by the men who had come out to meet them. Barmin opened the door for Rebrov. Rebrov, Shtaube, Olga, and Seryozha walked into the wide, dirty hallway, passed through the vestibule, and entered the foundry, most of which was taken up by an electric arc furnace, around which ten workers were bustling about. Fifteen more people were standing by a two-meter flask. Stuffing his hands into his pants pockets, Rebrov looked at the furnace and turned to Sergeyev.

"Give me your report."

Sergeyev coughed.

"So, Leonid Yakovlevich, yesterday at 12:45 we received 280 boxes of needles intended for disposable syringes and made by the West German firm Braun. Twenty-two thousand needles in every box. The total number of needles received was 6,160,000. We immediately unwrapped them and unloaded them into the furnace bath. The unloading was conducted continuously in three shifts and was completed today at 9:40. At 10:00, the furnace was ignited. At the present moment, everything is ready for the casting."

Rebrov looked at his watch.

"Show me a sample needle."

"Panteleyev!" Khlebnikov shouted.

A young worker ran in with an empty cardboard box labeled "Braun" and "The V.I. Lenin All-Union Children's Fund." There was a single plastic-wrapped needle at the bottom of the box. Rebrov took it out, unwrapped it, took off its plastic cap, looked at it, then threw it back into the box.

"You may begin."

Sergeyev waved his hand at the operator. The motor started running and the furnace began to slowly tip over. The new arrivals were given helmets, to which protective dark glasses were attached.

"Will the iron flow now?" Seryozha asked the grey-mustached worker who was helping him put on his helmet.

"Oh, it'll flow!" the worker chuckled. "But it's not iron! It's steel!"

"Is steel better than iron?"

"A lot better!" the worker put his hand on Seryozha's shoulder. "Take a look!"

A command came through on the radio, a loud bang rang out, and the steel flowed into the ladle.

"Woah! Cool!" Seryozha yelled.

"D'you wanna be a steelmaker?" the worker knelt down to Seryozha.

"Yeah!"

When all of the steel had flowed out, the ladle was dragged over to the flask and the casting began.

"When will it be ready?" Rebrov asked, removing his helmet.

"In ten hours," Sergeyev took the helmet from Rebrov.

Rebrov nodded and turned to Khlebnikov.

"So, Comrade Secretary. Let's go figure some stuff out."

They left the foundry, walked up the stairs to the second floor, and walked into the party committee secretary's large office. Pavlov got up from his desk and walked over to Rebrov. Rebrov silently proffered his hand and turned to Sergeyev.

"Lock the door and draw the blinds."

Khokhlov locked the door and Barmin drew the blinds. Sergeyev sat down at his desk. Rebrov, Shtaube, Olga, Seryozha, Barmin, Khlebnikov,

Khokhlov, Pavlov, Kozlov, Gelman, and Vyrin took their places at a long table typically used for meetings of the factory committee. Shtaube opened the briefcase, took out an envelope, and handed it to Sergeyev. Sergeyev took the envelope and pulled out a bundle of dollars.

"3k?"

"3,500," Shtaube replied.

"Now we're talkin' business!" Sergeyev smirked, putting the money away in his desk.

"I would earnestly ask that you not be late, Ivan Ivanovich," said Rebrov.

"I'll be on time," Sergeyev looked at his watch, "first though, let's hear from your little ruffian."

Everyone looked at Seryozha.

"Stand up, dear friend," Sergeyev took off his glasses and began wiping them with a handkerchief, "tell us about your exploits!"

Seryozha stood up and, lowering his head, began to speak.

"Well, I set off right after I got the call. An electric train. I got to Veshnyakov and then got on a bus. On the bus, I made it to . . . to the water tower."

"To the boiler," Rebrov interrupted.

"Mhmm. Then I found the street, then I found building number 7. Then I knocked and went in. A lady opened the door. And I said: I've come from Afanasy Fyodorovich. And she says: come in. A man was there and an old grandma too. She this . . . there, well, she was crying the whole time. And she was doing this with her hands . . ."

"Less detail," Sergeyev put on his glasses.

"Well, then I gave them the bag. To the lady. And he took it from her. And he says: let's go underground."

"Where?"

"Well, they had a basement there. And we go down. And there was a sauna and a pool. And different rooms. And there was a man down there who was kinda . . ."

"Hunchbacked?"

"Mhmm. And he had a nose that was kinda, well . . ."

"Broken."

"Mhmm. And there were two other ladies down there. And the first man gives the bag to the hunchback. And he takes the baltic out of the bag and puts it onto the talpik . . ."

"What, he had the talpik prepared in advance?" Sergeyev looked at Shtaube. Shtaube looked down.

"Mhmm, it was. It was on the table. And he pulled the lever and it flowed into the glass. And then they checked it on the sphere."

"And what numbers did it give?"

"7, 8."

Sergeyev sighed.

"Well, well. Keep going."

"Then the hunchback started to beat up the first guy. And the guy got down onto his knees and said, 'it was Pastukhov.' And one of the ladies also got down onto her knees. And then they started to beat me up. And they were asking about Pastukhov and about that . . . about the laboratory."

"And what were you doing?"

"Well I . . . was crying."

"What did you tell them?" Pavlov asked.

"I said that Pastukhov had left and that Samsikov was preparing the samples. Then they undressed me and started to hold me underwater in the pool. And the ladies were helping. And then I . . . well . . . I told them."

"About Pastukhov?"

Seryozha nodded. His listeners stirred disapprovingly.

"Save your reactions for later," Sergeyev looked at his watch. "Well? You spilled the beans about Pastukhov and then?"

"And then they put my clothes back on, counted the money again, and put it into my bag. And then the first lady wraps a rhombus up in some kind of, well, special paper and also puts it into my bag. And then the hunchback says: here's a lollipop for the road. And he made me suck . . . well . . . the place on the front of his body . . ."

Seryozha went quiet.

"I understand, I understand," Sergeyev looked at his watch again, "you spilled the beans about Pastukhov, you sucked the *front place*, you took the bag, then you left. Sit down. Zhenya! Please go say something so they start to break the flask. But a little more neatly this time . . ."

Khokhlov quickly got up from the table and left.

"All in all, then, my friends," Sergeyev smacked his hands against the desk, "our business is concluded. We do not wiiiiishhh to have any more dealings with you. I'll call Pastukhov today and, also today, right now, right after you get outta here, I'll order the closure of the northern. That's all!" he stood up.

"But Ivan Ivanovich, we'll compensate you, we'll . . ." Rebrov began.

"That's all! That's all!" Sergeyev waved his hand and began to walk over to the exit. "Take the casting and get outta here."

He left and the members of the factory administration started to follow him out. Shtaube slapped Seryozha in the face and Seryozha started crying.

"That's unnecessary," Pavlov shook his head. "The easiest thing to do is whip a child. You don't remember who said that? Gorky."

Everyone returned to the foundry. Six workers with sledgehammers broke the flask, which was then mounted to a steel platform. Soon the casing shivered and fell to pieces, revealing a burning, red-hot casting.

"Give me your report," said Rebrov.

"This means," Sergeyev coughed, "that using the strength of our enterprise and with the help of the staff of the State Zoological Museum, we have produced a stainless-steel casting of an itch mite ten thousand times larger than the actual bug. The weight of the casting is 1,800 kg."

Sergeyev nodded to Kozlov, who unfolded a piece of paper and began to read.

"'Itch mite (*Acarus siro*). Females are .3 mm long with round bodies, short legs, and leathery, furrowed integuments. The male is half as large. The female feeds on the skin of the afflicted individual, digging crooked passages, which are as long as 15 mm and can be seen through the skin as gray lines, into the stratum corneum. The eggs, which are .1 mm in length, are deposited into the passages and the female then digs small ventilation holes over them. The larva that hatches out of the eggs is devoid of all sexual characteristics and the last three segments of the abdomen, as well as all six segments of the legs, are not fully developed. The larva develops into a fully grown itching mite in two stages, first becoming a protonymph, then a teleonymph. The larvae and the protonymphs live in these passages, feeding on fluid from the tissue and the remnants of gnawed skin. They do not dig further passages. The protonymphs become teleonymphs, which then creep out onto the surface of the skin, usually at night when the afflicted individual is sleeping. At this point, some of the teleonymphs become males, which then mate with the female teleonymphs, or future female teleonymphs. Fertilized teleonymphs dig into the skin and become females. The males spend . . .'"

"Enough," Rebrov interrupted him. "Let's get loading."

Sergeyev waved his hand and the platform, hooked up to a crane, began to rise. The workers had already removed the broken pieces of the flask and cut the stragglers off of the casting, protecting themselves from the heat with shields.

"Oh, Leonid Yakovlevich, I forgot to tell you, we had a small unpleasantness with the chauffeur," Sergeyev frowned anxiously.

"What do you mean?"

"They sent the truck a while ago, but the chauffeur suddenly became ill: he vomited and nearly lost consciousness. He said that he'd eaten canned food this morning. Well, we called an ambulance. So, one of our people will drive you—Belkin or Sasha Yegorov."

"We'll find our own chauffeur," Rebrov walked forward, toward the closing gates of the foundry.

"As you wish," Sergeyev muttered angrily.

The crane lifted the platform out of the foundry and it dangled over the bed of the truck.

"Bring it on down!" a mustached worker shouted in Ukrainian and they brought the platform down into the bed of the truck.

Yakushev walked over to Rebrov.

"You'll drive the MAZ. Comrade Colonel will show you the way," said Rebrov. Yakushev nodded and got into the cabin. Shtaube got in with him.

Rebrov walked over to the ZIL and sat down in the driver's seat. Olga and Seryozha got into the back seat.

"How on earth . . ." Sergeyev frowned and turned red.

"Here's how, Comrade Sergeyev," Rebrov lowered the window, "do you think I've spent my whole life in an office?"

Khokhlov winked twice at Rebrov. Rebrov started the engine, turned sharply, drove over to the gates, and honked. The MAZ began to follow.

"Support, with the znedo on nine, Seryozha to take the sof," Rebrov said without turning around.

The gates opened, Rebrov turned left and accelerated sharply.

"So, what, did I turn out to be right, or what?" Yakushev smirked as he drove through the gates.

"Those Pastukhovian shit-asses!" Shtaube laughed. "Everyone's smeared! Pavlov, Sergeyev, and Fatass too! The assholes! The world's never seen anyone like 'em!"

"Now I understand why Radchenko put the map in the special safe."

"Oh, the dickheads! Oh, the pricks!" Shtaube laughed. "Barmin swore to God that Lebedev wouldn't meddle in Urengoy! And that business with the chauffeur! The retards!"

At 14:02, the truck drove up to the supermarket on Golubinskaya Street. A large crowd was noisily pushing their way through the recently opened doors of the store.

"Attention, comrades!" a voice resounded through a megaphone.

"I repeat that groceries will only be issued upon the presentation of one of two documents: one! a veteran's card! two! a Cheremushkinsky District Executive Committee ticket! In the event of the absence of either of these documents, no package of groceries shall be issued!"

"Why are they so late . . ." Shtaube yawned.

"As usual . . ." Yakushev drove around the crowd, turned, and began to drive toward the gates of the supermarket's inner courtyard.

"Where are these packages from?" Shtaube took out his segment and moved the teeth at two points.

"The Federal Republic of Germany. They wanted them to come by Christmas, but pushed it back for some reason."

"When do they not push it back?" Shtaube grinned.

Yakushev honked three times and the gates opened. The inner courtyard of the supermarket was completely full of people, who then moved off to the side to make way for the truck. The MAZ carefully drove in and stopped in front of a pile of sliced butter.

"Time to move!" Shtaube said to Yakushev, then got out of the truck and began making his way through the crowd.

The bed of the truck began to rise. Two forty-five-year-old women—twins named Masha and Marina who were dressed in identical grey quilted jackets, blue shawls, and rubber boots—walked up to Shtaube. Both of them were carrying a glass filled with clear liquid on a plate. Shtaube looked into the women's eyes, took the glass from Marina's plate, began to raise it to his lips, when, suddenly, he spat in Masha's face. Masha let forth a wild scream and, clutching at her face, fell down face-first.

"That's right, that's right!" Shtaube dropped the glass into the dirty snow, then lifted the other glass and sniffed at it.

"The whore deserves more than that," a fat fellow croaked, kneeling over Masha with a three-liter bottle. Someone removed the rubber cork and steaming acid flowed out over Masha's head. Someone else hit Marina in the head with an iron pipe and she fell down next to Masha.

"That's right, that's right!" Shtaube spat into the glass and threw it violently at the face of someone standing nearby. The man grabbed at his face and turned away. At the same moment, the crimson-red casting sank down into the pile of sliced butter with a hiss and was engulfed in steam. "That's right, that's right," Shtaube made a complex motion with his hand.

Eleven people lifted up a concrete slab and laid it down on top of Masha and Marina. Sixteen people carried over a massive fireproof cabinet and put it on top of the slab. They helped Shtaube up onto the slab, then he climbed up on top of the cabinet and straightened up, leaning onto his cane. Everyone went quiet. Shtaube pulled a piece of paper out of his jacket pocket, unfolded it, then crumpled it up and tossed it away . . .

"That's right," he pronounced exhaustedly, grabbing on to his cane with both hands, "standing on one leg, propping myself up . . . You know, it's difficult to imagine modern life without rubber, without caoutchouc. We wear rubberized coats and rubber boots and we use rubber hoses. Sometimes we even wear rubberized diving suits. Without caoutchouc, we wouldn't have road transportation, aviation, electrical engineering, or mechanical engineering. Caoutchouc means tires, wire insulation, the blimps of balloons, and thousands upon thousands of other irreplaceable things. On the other hand, the multifaceted world of synthetic resins. And perhaps the most fascinating among these synthetic resins are ion-exchange resins or even just ion-exchangers . . ." Shtaube fell silent for a moment, frowned in concentration, then passed his hand across his face. "Who among us hasn't dreamed while standing before a map: how good it would be to go to the Caucasus, to the Arctic, to Antarctica, to the Karakum Desert, or, for example, to Cologne. This is very interesting, of course. But if you become acquainted with the biographies of great travelers, you'll learn that long before they voyaged to distant lands, they traveled through their own countries quite a bit. In one's native land, in which, at first glance, everything appears to be already known, there

The MAZ carefully drove in and stopped in front of a pile of sliced butter.

always turns out to be many new and interesting things in which to delve. The main thing in travelling is the ability to see and to observe. For example, not far from here is a sign on a post next to a bus stop: 'Young family looking to rent apartment at reasonable price. We guarantee cleanliness and order. Call: 145 18 06.' And I recalled Dmitry Ivanovich Mendeleyev. Organic geology is a fascinating discipline. She's a modest, an incredibly modest *laboress*. Or Lieutenant General Karbyshev. Fascist pigs tortured this brave Soviet general in the dungeons of multiple concentration camps. On the night of February 18, 1945, the fascists led him into the courtyard of the prison at Mauthausen and poured cold water onto him in minus-twelve-degree weather until the body of this Soviet patriot had turned into a block of ice. Or the late Triassic Period, brachiopods, communist inventory number . . . and also, basically, the fact that as the temperature of any body approaches absolute zero, its change in entropy, its inherent properties also change and begin to approach zero. But . . . no!!! No!!! No-o-o!!! Fucking! No-o! She squelched it! Her reeking cunt! When they boiled her three children alive! Alive! Is that how they imagine change? No?! I'm asking you! Is that how they imagine universality? Imagine boiled children? Imagine the fucked? What? Haven't you heard? About Antonina Lvovna Mandavoshina! First, she trembled her twat all across Kharkov! Then on the road to Volokolamsk! Then in the heroic capital of our Motherland, the city of Moscow! She was eating shit for twenty years on a committee of shitty, fucking, pissing, dick-sucking Soviet mothers and daughters! Whatever three times thirty-three is, that's how many times she got fucked! Fucked down to her skeleton by cocks! She showed them all her shaggy, sour, wormy pussy! Fucking medals! An order! Ranks and merits! Fucking honor! Esteem! And I shit and pissed on your hump! I shit and pissed on your sweaty tits! I shit and pissed on your wet-assed mother, then I fucked her, you dirty-assed cunt! I shit and pissed on your medals! I shit and pissed on your order! I shit on your boiled children! I shit! I shit! Shi-i-it! Shi-i-it!!!" He put his hand over his pale face, was silent for a moment, shrugged his shoulders, and then began to speak

at the corpse's pale face. "All his life, he suffered from a severe form of sinusitis. Bring me the chisel and the hammer."

They handed him a narrow chisel and a wooden hammer. With only a few strokes, Shtaube opened up the maxillary sinus cavities in the corpse's face. A greenish pus slowly flowed from the holes.

"Left and right!" Shtaube said loudly. A girl came up to the table from the left and a boy came up to the table from the right. They quickly took off all their clothes. Leaning over the corpse, Shtaube sucked the pus from the left maxillary cavity, walked up to the girl, pressed his lips to her lips, and released the pus from his mouth into her mouth. Then he sucked the pus from the corpse's right maxillary cavity, walked up to the boy, and released the pus from his mouth into the boy's mouth.

"Pass it on," said Shtaube and began to walk through the crowd toward the service entrance. Two lines began to form, one in front of the boy and one in front of the girl. A porter and a saleswoman were waiting in front of the service entrance. They moved to the side in order to let Shtaube into a dimly lit hallway. Rebrov handed Shtaube a bottle of potassium permanganate solution. He grabbed it, took a sip, rinsed his mouth carefully, then spat.

"The ropes haven't been chosen," Rebrov said.

"I'm not Oleg Popov!" Shtaube said irritably and, still rinsing out his mouth, began to move down the hallway.

"I warned you," Rebrov began to follow him, kneading at his cigarette.

Following after them, the porter and the saleswoman bolted the door closed behind them.

"To the right, Henry Ivanych," Rebrov prompted and they walked into a space lined with barrels of pickled vegetables. In the corner, Olga, Seryozha, and Yakushev were sitting next to two open packages of groceries and snacking.

"Fuck!" Shtaube threw the bottle into the corner. "I burned my whole mouth . . ."

He knocked a stone off of the lid of one of the barrels, moved the lid to the side, scooped up a handful of cabbage brine, and drank thirstily. The saleswoman locked the door and got down onto her knees. The porter unbuttoned his quilted jacket, then lifted up his dirty sweater. There were traces of recently healed burns on his chest and stomach. The saleswoman let forth a sob, then wept in silence.

"Yes . . . the anti-latest . . ." Shtaube took a stick of nibbled salami from Seryozha and bit into it.

"What to show now?" Yakushev smirked, chewing a cookie.

"The clothes?" Rebrov asked the saleswoman. She pointed at a wooden box in the corner.

"Deal with the clothes, Henry Ivanych," Rebrov gave the porter one hundred dollars, took a destithread out of his wallet, got down onto his knees in front of the saleswoman, and put one of the destithread's loops around her two upper front teeth and the other end around his own. Seryozha walked over, started the spheria, and carefully lowered it onto the barely visible destithread. The spheria rolled along the destithread, buzzing weakly.

"Akharan, akharan, akharan," Rebrov pronounced, not moving his teeth.

"Khatara, khatara, khatara," the saleswoman responded. The spheria moved to her lips, then moved back to Rebrov's lips. Shtaube took a heap of clothes out of the box, took off the colonel's uniform he was wearing, and changed into a sweater and wool trousers.

"Agakakh, agakakh, agakakh," Rebrov pronounced.

"Khanaka, khanaka, khanaka," the saleswoman replied. The spheria moved to the center of the destithread, then moved back to the saleswoman's lips. Shtaube put on a short sheepskin coat, felt boots, and an ushanka hat. The lock clicked faintly and the door swung open, knocking over the saleswoman. Four men wearing bulletproof vests burst into the room with assault rifles.

"KGB! Everyone down!"

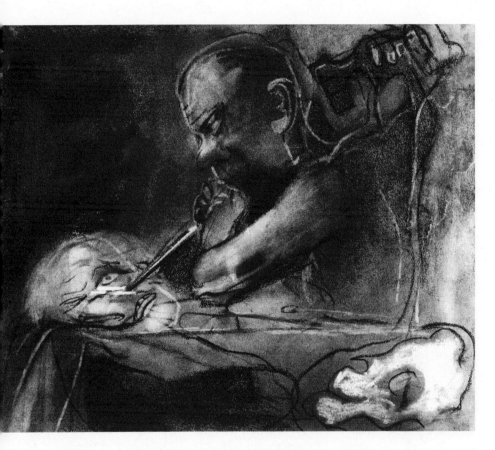

With only a few strokes, Shtaube opened up the maxillary sinus cavities in the corpse's face.

"Akharan, akharan, akharan," Rebrov pronounced, not moving his teeth.

Rebrov, the porter, Yakushev, and the saleswoman fell to the floor. Shtaube raised his hands into the air.

"Get down!" they pushed him and he fell, his leg sticking up into the air.

Olga pressed Seryozha tightly to her body and pinched him.

"My darlings! My darlings! They kidnapped me and my son! They tortured us! Oh God!"

"Mommy! Mommy!" Seryozha sobbed, grabbing on to her neck.

Two more came in with pistols and handcuffs.

"Arrest them! Tie them up right now! Right now!" Olga sobbed, covering her bag with Seryozha's body. "There are three more! In the commodity expert's office! They're drinking in there! Go now!"

"There's no rush," a man in a leather jacket holding a pistol pronounced calmly, "first let go of the little brat. You're his mom like I'm his dad. I'm counting to one."

Seryozha moved off to the side.

"Now get down on the ground with your hands over your head."

Olga got down onto the brine-slick floor. They put handcuffs on everyone except for Seryozha.

"Novikov's with me, the rest of you go to the commodity expert," the man in the leather jacket ordered. One man with an assault rifle stayed with him and the rest of them left the room.

"Are those needles or what?" the man in the leather jacket nodded at the box of clothes. The gunman turned to the box and the man in the leather jacket shot him in the back of the neck.

The gunman fell. In the hallway, a long burst of automatic fire rang out.

"Hello?" the man in the leather jacket pointed his pistol at the door.

"Flight," someone said behind the door.

"Union," he replied, letting another gunman in. "So?"

"We have a situation!" the gunman smiled nervously and shot him in the face. Bloody chunks flew onto the wall and the man in the leather jacket fell, not having had time to shoot back. The gunman pulled a key out of his jacket pocket and winked at Seryozha.

"Let's do it now . . . where are your people?"

Seryozha pointed at Rebrov, Olga, and Shtaube. The gunman threw the key to Seryozha and shot the porter, the saleswoman, and Yakushev in three short bursts.

"Why did you shoot Galya?!" Olga got up onto her knees. "Nothing better to do with your bullets? Asshole! Puh!" she spat on the gunman.

"Leave through the main hall, they have the back and the wine section covered," the gunman mumbled, then replaced his clip and ran out. Seryozha took off Olga's handcuffs, then they both took off Rebrov and Shtaube's handcuffs. Cabbage brine flowed out of the holey barrels and the spheria rolled around on the floor, buzzing softly.

"Oy . . . I can't . . . Forgive me . . ." Shtaube went into the corner, unbuttoned his pants, and squatted down, lifting up the hem of his sheepskin coat. He had diarrhea. Rebrov picked up the destithread and unlooped it from the saleswoman's teeth.

"We have to be quick!"

"What a bastard!" Olga pulled her pistol out of her bag, put it into her waistband, and put on a fur coat. "That's Zlotnikov for you!"

"Zlotnikov plows for Pastukhov," with his cane, Shtaube pulled over the porter's knit hat, which had flown off of his head, and wiped himself with it. "The cunt talked a lotta shit and everyone believed him . . ."

"Quickly! Quickly!" Rebrov peeked through the door. Shtaube pulled up his pants and limped over. They left and moved down the hallway. Many dead gunmen and one dead man in civilian clothes were lying in front of the commodity expert's office. Slightly further down the hall, a fat saleswoman who had been terribly wounded and now had only half a face was lying on the ground wearing a white lab coat, her fingers clutching at a bit of broken armature and her urine-filled felt boots trembling weakly. A gunman and a young saleswoman holding a bloody axe stood in front of the doors to the main hall.

"Let's move! Before they cotton on," the gunman undid the bolt on the door. Olga spat in his face.

"Idiot!" he laughed, wiping away the spit. The saleswoman looked spitefully at Olga and opened the door. Rebrov, Shtaube, Olga, and Seryozha walked into the main hall. There were a lot of people in the hall and veterans were waiting for their humanitarian aid packages in three long lines. To the left of the stalls, people were fighting, women were screaming, and men were shouting: a woman was lying next to the wall and a community support officer and a policeman were holding ammonia to her nose. By the exit, people were trading groceries from the packages they'd just received. Rebrov squeezed through the crowd, making a path for the others.

"Help me, son!" a short, fat disabled man on crutches grabbed Rebrov's arm. "I can't carry it on my own! Help me for Christ's sake!"

"Not for Christ's sake, brother," Shtaube grabbed one side of the disabled man's package and Rebrov grabbed the other, "but for the glory of the Soviet soldier!"

"Thank you, brothers, oh thank you!" the disabled man smiled excitedly and hobbled after them. "Where did you serve, my friend?"

"On the 1st Belorussian Front," Shtaube cheerfully leaned on his cane as he walked. "Started out near Prokhorovka and ended up in Berlin."

"Did you write your name on the Reichstag?"

"I wrote my name, then I took a shit between the columns. A shit straight from the heart."

"Were you a tankman?"

"No way. I was a God of war."

"Ah, in the artillery! Of course! Artillery men, Stalin gave the order!"

"Artillery men, the Fatherland is ca-a-alling!" Shtaube sang.

Rebrov, Olga, and Seryozha loudly joined in.

"From a hundred thousand batteries, for the tears of our mothers, for our Motherland, fire, fi-i-ire!"

The crowd parted in front of them. They left the store.

"And now, have you heard, the West Germans send us packages!" the disabled man laughed animatedly.

"Yeah. They want to shut us up with sausage," Shtaube looked around warily. "Well, fuck them . . ."

They dropped the package into the snow, maneuvered around the crowd gathered outside of the store, and got into a red Moskvich with a black and yellow disabled sticker. The ZIL was parked next to the news stand and a group of policemen and officers in civilian clothes were bustling around it. Rebrov started the engine, rolled out onto Golubinskaya, and drove away carefully.

"Did we get away?" Olga put her pistol into her bag and pulled out a cigarette case.

"Not so fast, Olga Vladimirovna," Shtaube squinted through the window. "They don't take whupass well."

"Did you lose the shuttle, Seryozha?" Rebrov licked at his dry lips.

"Nah," Seryozha pulled out the shuttle.

"Give it to me," Olga took the shuttle, put it into the pocket of her fur coat, and lit up. "Why didn't you mention Zlotnikov, Vitya?"

"Because Radchenko didn't personally know Solovyova."

"And you weren't completely sure?" Shtaube turned to him.

"And I wasn't completely sure."

"That means it's . . . a wrap?"

"It's a wrap," Rebrov grabbed Olga's cigarette and took a drag.

"Live and learn!" Shtaube smiled maliciously. "But you pay with your health!"

"We didn't have a choice, Henry Ivanovich. The risk was justified and we'd already examined the segments."

"What about the segments . . . we got an 8 in the allotment. Hard to know what to believe . . ."

"Trust the instructions, Henry Ivanovich. Everyone's attention, please: we have to be incredibly attentive at the station."

"Mimicry?" Olga asked.

"6, 3. And very, very lightly . . ."

"What do you mean lightly!" Shtaube muttered, turning away.

At 14:55, they arrived at the Kazansky Station.

"Porter!" Rebrov shouted as he got out of the car. One porter extracted himself from a group of his colleagues and wheeled a trolley over to the car.

"Train 56, please," Rebrov opened the trunk.

"The Yenisei? Alright . . ." the porter yanked the metal box with the intermediate block, the suitcase with the mother liquid, and the knapsack out of the trunk and put them onto his trolley. Rebrov grabbed the attaché case and Shtaube grabbed the briefcase. The porter pushed the trolley away quickly.

"Let's get some ice cream!" Seryozha grabbed Olga's hand.

"You can't eat ice cream in the winter, Seryozha," Rebrov said drily.

As they approached the platform, the porter who had gone ahead turned around.

"Which car?"

Rebrov pulled out the tickets.

"The seventh. Seats 9-12."

In front of the wagon, a curly-haired Tartar conductress came up to them with a smile to check their tickets.

"All the way to Krasnoyarsk? Wonderful! These days, it's planes, planes, planes! Are you smuggling diamonds maybe?" she nodded at the metal box the porter was handling.

"Worse. Camera equipment," Rebrov took the tickets back from her.

"To make a movie about us?" she laughed, showing off her gold teeth. "It's about time someone did!"

The porter took the baggage into their compartment. Rebrov gave him six rubles. Nine minutes later, the train began to move.

"Thanks be to you, oh God," Shtaube crossed himself.

"We're off!" Seryozha closed the window curtain.

Someone knocked on the door.

"It's open!" Rebrov said loudly. The conductress came in and sat down on the edge of the divan.

"You get settled in alright?" she didn't stop smiling as she laid a leather folder with a little pocket for tickets onto her knees.

"Entirely," Rebrov nodded, giving her the tickets.

"What's the situation with the restaurant car, my sweet?" Shtaube asked.

"Better than your situation in Moscow," she flipped over the tickets and put them in the pocket of the folder, "we've got caviar, balyk, hodge-podge, and rotisserie chicken. Cognac and champagne too."

"Wonderful!" Shtaube slapped his knee.

Rebrov gave her ten rubles.

"For bedsheets and tea."

"And you keep the change," Olga smiled.

"Thank you," the conductress took the money. "No joke—are you off to make a movie?"

"No joke."

"About love?"

"About ecology."

"U-g-g-g-h! And here I was thinking . . ."

"You don't like our subject?" Rebrov exchanged a look with Olga.

"We're already up to our necks in ecology," the conductress stood up. "As if we don't already have enough clean air in Siberia! Go to the taiga and breathe in all the fresh air you want. I'll bring you your tea in a half hour . . ."

She left. Shtaube locked the door immediately.

"Enough! Let's chow down! I'm dyin'!"

"To the restaurant car?" Rebrov touched his mustache distractedly.

"We've got so many groceries, what do we need the restaurant car for!" Olga pulled the knapsack out from under the table.

•

An hour later, their refection was complete. Seryozha helped Olga throw away all of the chicken bones, egg shells, and bread crusts. The conductress came in with tea.

"Wonderful!" Shtaube wiped his hands with a napkin.

"I could drink gallons of this stuff," Seryozha said.

"Cheers!" the conductress laughed, distributing the cups.

"How long will it be to Krasnoyarsk, darling?" Shtaube poured cognac into his tea from a silver flask.

"Almost three days."

"Enough to drive you insane," Olga shook her head, "we'll really get sick of trains . . ."

"Oh no, you won't," the conductress took away the bag of garbage, "everyone gets off at Gorky and Kazan, so we'll be the only ones left, we can even play soccer if you want. We'll drink tea and play cards."

"Well, well!" Shtaube winked at her. She walked out. Everyone looked at Rebrov.

"Iro, iro . . ." he muttered wearily, unbuttoning the collar of his shirt.

"It's my job to warn you," Shtaube sipped his tea, "it was all iro with the golutvin too."

"Enough, enough, enough!" Olga smacked her palm against the table, spilling their tea. "Are you enjoying yourself? I have to sit here, bat my eyes at you, and ask over and over again: oh yes, what would *you* prefer?"

"What do you mean by prefer?" Shtaube frowned.

"Tell me, Henry Ivanych, am I your daughter maybe? Or your stepmother? Do I have your permission to cry? To curtsy? Or, to do this?" she asked, making a complex motion with her hands.

"Olga Vladimirovna . . ." Rebrov sighed.

"Iro is for you what my sickness is for me! Like that hospital in Sokol! And am I a nurse?! Or a cleaning lady? Keep moving, Olenka, keep moving!"

"We were working together! I wasn't the one who took those figures down from the ceiling!" Shtaube exclaimed angrily.

"You mean I made them up with Galya? Who's now dead?! Pulled them out of a hat, then slipped them in? Fantastic!"

"This has nothing to do with you!"

"Of course, it doesn't! Nothing has anything to do with me! I'm supposed to pull the trigger and then sing like a beluga during the allotment! Push the triangle, Olenka! Move it to 18, Olenka! Enough! Enough! Enough!" pushing Seryozha off to the side, she started to leave, but Rebrov grabbed her arm, pulled her over to him, and covered her mouth. Olga began to sob and pulled away from him. Seryozha fell down at her feet. Shtaube put the flask into her mouth and she choked down the cognac, coughing protractedly and convulsively.

"More," she said, now calm and sitting next to Seryozha. Shtaube handed her the flask. Wiping away her tears, she drank thirstily, then handed the flask back to Rebrov. He sniffed it, had a swallow, and handed it to Shtaube, who screwed the lid back on.

"Sleep, Olga Vladimirovna," Rebrov stroked her hand. "We all need to sleep. To restore ourselves."

Olga woke up to Seryozha's cry, grabbed her pistol from underneath her pillow, and pointed it at the door. The compartment was dark. The train was moving fast and their car was rocking from side to side. Sleeping on the top bunk, Seryozha was moaning and crying out weakly. Olga looked down. Rebrov and Shtaube were sleeping. She put away her pistol, pushed her blanket off to the side, and moved over to Seryozha's couchette.

"Drive . . . drove!" Seryozha mumbled, before he jerked awake. "Who is it?"

"It's me, honey."

"I'm afraid, Ol," Seryozha squeezed himself against Olga.

"Oh darling, you're trembling . . ."

"I had a dream . . . a scary dream . . . that we were at our dacha and

"I'm afraid, Ol," Seryozha squeezed himself against Olga.

you sent me to this . . . sent me down to the basement, to get the rod and, well, the rod fell down at the allotment . . . and I go down and you're yelling at me where to go . . . and the passages down there are so narrow, they're made of dirt, and larvae spill onto me and I can't breathe. They're as sticky and as fat as pigs . . ."

"Darling," Olga stroked his sweaty forehead, "there aren't any larvae."

"Are we still . . . going?"

"We're going, going, going off to faraway lands. Sleep," she looked at the glowing dial of her watch. "It's past two."

"Are we going to Siberia, Ol?"

"Yes, to Siberia."

"Is it big?"

"Very big."

"Have you been there before?"

"Once. At a training camp in Magadan. In the summer, though."

"Olenka."

"What, darling?"

"Suck me off."

Olga touched his erect penis and kissed him on the temple.

"Now?"

"Mhmm . . ." He threw his blanket off to the side and pulled off his underpants. Olga put her bosom onto his knees, brought his penis into her mouth, and began to rhythmically move her head. He helped her, as he stared at the dark ceiling. Soon, he shuddered and froze.

Olga wiped at her lips with the palm of her hand, rose up, and kissed him on the cheek.

"My little one . . . you fed your Olenka. You're not going to cry out anymore?"

He shook his head.

"Then I'll go back to my bed. It's not too cold for you to sleep?"

He shook his head, then Olga went back to her couchette and got under the blanket.

"The train's rocking like a boat! Hold on to your pillow!"

Seryozha was already sleeping.

They woke up early. Had a long breakfast while the train was stopped in Kazan.

"Fifty years have passed, but their ugly mugs are still the same," Shtaube sipped his tea and looked at the people on the platform.

"You've been here before?" Rebrov asked.

"But of course!" he counterfeited a tearful expression and began to speak with a strong Tartar accent. "The evacuation of Boarding School No. 18—the Comrade Makarenko School—doesn't matter to us, brothers: sanatorium, crematorium, no one cares what-atorium so long as it's free! We lived here six months, then moved on to Ashgabat. When we got there, we had bloody diarrhea for a week."

"You went to boarding school?" Seryozha asked as he shelled a hard-boiled egg. "What about your parents?"

"They killed my parents, Seryozha."

"The Germans?"

"Gypsies killed my parents on July 6, 1941, Seryozha," Shtaube finished his tea. "And to kill someone's parents, Seryozha, is a great sin."

"But what about . . . Leningrad?"

"What about Leningrad?"

"Well, the Siege of Leningrad. I thought you were in the Siege."

"I was at the znedo of the Siege, Seryozha. And sometimes I was in Drogobych."

"And your parents?"

"What about my parents?"

"Well, were your parents in Drogobych too?"

"They were. Sort of."

"What do you mean?" Seryozha took a bite of his egg.

"Only the upper bit. The strebon."

"Ahhh . . . uh-huh . . ."

The train began to move. Soon, the conductress came in with their tea.

"Here we are! There're only ten passengers left in the whole car. Give me some of your empty cups . . ."

When she left, Olga locked the compartment, put her pistol on the table and took a rag, oil, and a ramrod out of the knapsack. Rebrov went up to the upper bunk and immersed himself in his notes. Shtaube put two cubes of sugar into his tea and started to stir it with a spoon.

"I've wanted to ask you for a long time, Olga Vladimirovna, what's the caliber of your weapon?"

"It's a 9-mm," Seryozha responded quickly, "the trigger mechanism is self-cocking, the slide is free, it has a flag-style safety, the magazine holds ten rounds, it has a swift sight, and the handle was handmade from beech."

"Did you hear that, Comrade Rebrov?" Shtaube stood up on one leg and began to imitate Stalin. "Yet sam-how we have cam ta be distrestful of our yith!"

Rebrov didn't reply.

"A second question, then: why is it, darling, that when you, so to speak, shoot your weapon, you don't hold it with two hands, like our glorious police officers, but with one?"

"That's how I was taught, Henry Ivanych," Olga removed the bolt. "Cops hold their guns with two hands because that's the only way they can hit their targets with such crappy weapons. At ten paces, a Makar gives you a spread of half a meter. They're lumpy, inaccurate, poorly balanced, and they'll dislocate your wrist. With my gun, I'll hit the ampoule of a light bulb at ten paces . . ."

"Stop! Stop!" Rebrov exclaimed. "What did Borisov Station used to be called?"

"Karpilovo," Shtaube replied.

"Fantastic!" Rebrov laughed. "On my grid, that's in the blue."

"That can't be!" Shtaube raised himself up.

Rebrov showed him the battered notebook.

"The fortieth. And according to the allotment, as I'm sure you remember, it was 7."

Shtaube took the notebook and began to move his lips.

"The fortieth . . . so . . ."

Olga attached the rag bolt to the ramrod.

"Well, so what. We're still gonna have to work around it."

"But we don't have to go all the way to Krasnoyarsk. We can stop seventy kilometers before the city."

"In Tarutino?"

"In Kozulka."

Olga applied oil to the rag bolt and then pushed the ramrod into the barrel.

"You know, when a kitty finds a turtle without its shell, first it sniffs at it, and then it really presses its nose into the thing. Or when people fight over who'll do the dishes: one person really, really stamps their feet and waves around a hose with a metal nozzle, and, even if they walk on the kerskian, the other person doesn't fall, but jumps up and puts the grate into place. It's simple and it's reliable."

Rebrov's watch showed 23:46 and a blue lamp was shining in the compartment. Olga and Seryozha were sleeping on the top bunks. Shtaube poured what was left of the cognac into two glasses.

"Private property, Viktor Valentinovich, is a mere pretext. The party apparatus is, of course, a terrifying force, but it's not without its limits. That's especially noticeable now. What do you know about the Germans? Gas chambers for subhumans? Pea soup with sausages? When they were persecuting us, what was the accordionist singing? Don't worry, recruit, the Germans will squash you like rotten fruit!"

"I'm not inclined to view the party apparatus as an exclusively reactionary force," Rebrov took the glass of cognac, drained it in a single gulp, and bit into an apple. "In our current situation, the communists are capable of positive, truly democratic approaches. The reverse is also true: the democrats, or perhaps it would be better to say quasi-democrats, have a totalitarian approach to authority. The Germans don't frighten me, true, but they also don't inspire much calm in me. Remember Goebbels as a student: evil is nothing more than a disparity between being and obligation."

"So, you probably think that Stalin was a terrible bastard and not a great reformer?"

"In terms of the spiritual rebirth and national revival of Russia, Stalin did more than all of the leaders before him combined. As a Christian and a healthy-minded individual, I welcome Stalin's reforms. As an economist and a geopolitician, I also welcome them. But, as a Russian intellectual, I can't help but condemn these reforms. And notice the word I use—reforms! I don't condemn Stalin himself. Remember what Berdyaev said: Russian communism represents, on the one hand, the appearance of a global, international phenomenon, but, on the other hand, a Russian, national phenomenon. Lenin, alas, did not understand this."

"He did, however, have a wonderful understanding of Germany's counterpartship."

"About which Stalin could only guess. Confused, but correct, guesses."

"I still hate Stalin." Shtaube took a drink of cognac, "his inconsistency, his softness, his reluctance to assert his agency in the resolution of important issues, his betting on a union of the intelligentsia and the peasantry and against the proletariat . . . the shithead! the fucking shithead! The most horrible thing is when a gifted person isn't able to bring their talent to fruition. To have beheaded the Red Army at the beginning of the thirties would have been an incredible accomplishment, but to have done so in '37 or '40 was a terrible crime! The liquidation of the well-to-do peasantry, the robbery of peasant farms, the creation of collective farm corvées, all of this is brilliant, fantastic, but . . ."

"But to have done this at the end of the twenties was absurd!" Rebrov chuckled.

"Of course! Wait ten years, let the boors get fat, let 'em fill their coffers . . ."

"And then—take it all away! If he'd started doing all of this in '36, the effect of the depeasantization would've been five or ten times greater. The Russian peasantry began to have some form of economic independence only in 1910, then war, revolution, Lenin and Trotsky's idiotic prodrazvyorstka, a brief pause, then, finally, collectivization . . ."

"And the national question?! As was always the case with Stalin, it was conceived of brilliantly, but brought to life haphazardly! And you blame Bismarck!"

"Not Bismarck, but the Prussian philistines who emasculated and perverted his ideas. Two of those philistines, Molotov and Bukharin, deserve universal contempt. Stalin should've listened to Zinoviev's advice instead of Kaganovich's. If his life had played out differently, we would live under a different state. Zinoviev's path through the labyrinths of power is just as tragic as Himmler's: both rays of bright dimmed by dusky bureaucratic lenses."

"It's unbelievable!" Shtaube was peeling an apple with a penknife. "None of these turkeys allowed themselves to reach out their hand, to lean on a trusty shoulder, or even to ask for advice! What the fuck is that? Egoism or fear?"

"It's obtromoan," Rebrov replied after brief reflection.

The train began to brake and city lights flashed outside the window.

"Sverdlovsk," Shtaube looked out the window.

"You've been here too?"

"Not once," Shtaube laughed. "It took me sixty-six years to get here! That's Russia for you! Let's drink to that!"

"To a road that's sixty-six years long?"

"Exactly!" Shtaube took a bottle of vodka out of the knapsack and started to open it. "I've always liked these insane Russian distances. They're somehow . . . arousing, aren't they?"

"I'm just the opposite: they oppress me. By the way, Henry Ivanych, have you looked at the band?"

"But of course! Early this morning, when you went to bathe. The cone is in the tolerance."

"What numbers did it give?"

"4, 7. The root isn't visible."

Rebrov nodded satisfactorily and pushed his glass over to Shtaube.

"Well, in that case, it's no sin to take a drink."

At 9:12, the conductress woke them up with a knock on the door. Rebrov opened it, then she came in and put a teapot and glasses on the table.

"Good morning! How could you sleep through Omsk? There was so much being sold on the platform! It was bananas! Wolf hats for one hundred rubles, Orenburg shawls for just twenty-five, white felt boots . . . everyone was losing their minds! That's what you oughta film!"

"Another time, I guess . . ." Shtaube muttered hoarsely, picking up his prosthesis off of the floor.

"What river is that?" Seryozha looked down from the top bunk.

"The Irtysh."

"And why didn't it freeze?"

"It flows so quickly that it never freezes. In a half hour, I'll bring you some more tea."

She left, loudly slamming the door behind her.

"They have the heat on too high!" Olga threw off her blanket and stretched out.

"You can't break bones with too much heat, Olenka," sitting on the divan, Shtaube poured the tea into a glass and took a sip. "Ah, glorious."

Rebrov got dressed, pulled out the attaché case, opened it, and sniffed at the bag containing a slice of Leontiev's chest.

"What? Did it rot?" Shtaube asked.

"No. Everything's in order," Rebrov put away the attaché case and took out a towel, a tube of toothpaste, and a toothbrush. "After breakfast, let's be ready for a small allotment. Seryozha will be the pointer."

•

They ate lunch in the half-empty restaurant car. While waiting for dessert, Olga began to play Napoleon's Tomb solitaire on the table, Rebrov smoked while looking out the window, Seryozha fiddled with his Rubik's cube, and Shtaube read out loud from Alexey Tolstoy's *The Silver Prince*:

"'Many servants, dressed in velvet caftans of a violet color with gold embroidery, stood in front of the sovereign, bowed to him at the waist, and set off for the food in rows of two. They soon returned carrying several hundred roasted swans on golden platters. When the swans had been eaten, the servants left the chamber two-by-two and returned with three-hundred baked peacocks, whose fluffy tails waved above each platter as if they were fans. After the peacocks, the servants brought out kulebyaki, kurniki, pies with meat and cheese, blini of every possible variety, moon-shaped pirozhki, and fritters. And still, the supper continued. They first laid out all sorts of galantines on the tables; they then brought out cranes in a spiced sauce, brined cocks with ginger, boneless ducks, and chicken with cucumbers. They then brought out various broths and two different kinds of ukha: blackened-chicken and saffron-chicken. After the ukha, they brought out grouse with plums, goose and millet, and greyhen with saffron. On yon day, the Tsar's chefs truly distinguished themselves. Never before had they so distinguished themselves with lemon balms, rabbit kidneys, or Crucian carp with lamb. The rabbits in noodles were also fine and delicious and the guests, no matter how stuffed they may have been, left behind not a single quail in garlic sauce nor a single lark with onions and saffron.' There you go, Olga Vladimirovna. And you say that it's an *okay* cuisine."

"Didn't quite nail it," Olga started to pick up the cards. The waitress brought coffee and stale pastries. Rebrov paid immediately and tipped her a ruble.

"You'll break your teeth on those," Olga took a bite from a pastry and immediately spat it out.

"Distribute 'em to the beggars at stops between stations," Shtaube yawned.

The train started to brake.

"This is Novosibirsk," Rebrov looked at his watch. "We should go out and get a breath of fresh air."

"I'm gonna sleep," said Shtaube, leaning on his cane.

They returned to their compartment, Shtaube lay down with a book, Olga, Rebrov, and Seryozha put on warm clothes and went out onto the platform to get a breath of fresh air.

"It's so cold!" Seryozha pressed himself to Olga.

The conductress stood off to the side, spitting out sunflower seeds.

"Y'really think it's cold? It's only minus twenty-eight. It's cold when it gets to be less than minus forty."

A man in a tattered short sheepskin coat walked up to her.

"Sell me some vodka, dear woman."

"We don't sell vodka," she spat out a shell.

"I'll give you thirty."

She turned away. The man walked away, his felt boots creaking. A grandpa in a quilted jacket walked up to the conductress and untied his canvas bag.

"Hey there, darlin', have a look at this!"

There was a pig's head in the bag.

"Stew him in a big ole pot and till Easter, ye'll eat a lot!" the grandpa rhymed with a smile.

"When'd they cut it off?" the conductress touched the head.

"Day before yesterday. Ye can have the bag with it for nothin'."

The conductress thought for a moment, then pulled a bottle of vodka out of her pocket and handed it to the old man.

"Now we're talkin'!" he tucked it away and walked off.

"This stop will last fifteen minutes!" the conductress winked at Seryozha, picked up the bag, and got onto the train.

"This station's kinda nice," Olga looked at the station building, "better than what we have in Norilsk. Shall we have a look?"

"We shall abstain," Rebrov lit up.

"Ah, you're too cautious Vitenka!" Olga took the cigarette from his mouth, took a drag, and, throwing back her head, blew smoke up into the air.

Seventy-two kilometers away from Achinsk, at Bogotol Station, three railway men in quilted jackets and yellow vests sat down in compartment no. 7.

"Everyone at the depot was sayin' you were on maternity leave!" the oldest of the three workers smiled at the conductress. "And we thought, 'can it really be that our last countrywoman has run away from the Yenisei? Who'll pour us our tea?'"

"I'll pour you your tea, but first shake off your boots!" the conductress grinned.

Standing in the hallway, Rebrov winked at Olga. She opened her bag, pulled out a hand mirror and a tube of lipstick, and began to apply it to her lips.

"Even without that, Olenka, you look like Sophia Loren," Shtaube remarked, lying down on the other side of the compartment.

"The capitalistic is on 7," Olga said.

Shtaube raised himself up with a grunt. Seryozha immediately got down from the top bunk and put his Rubik's cube into the rucksack.

"Is the train stuffed to the gills again?" a younger railwayman asked the conductress.

"There're only twelve people onboard! Choose any compartment, I'll bring you tea in a sec."

"That's what I'm talkin' about!" the workers walked into the first compartment.

Rebrov walked into their compartment and sat down by the open door.

"I thought you'd be getting on at Zertsaly," the conductress poured boiling water out from the tender.

"You wouldn't believe the drifts here, impossible to shovel away!

Seryozha fiddled with his Rubik's cube, and Shtaube read out loud from Alexey Tolstoy's *The Silver Prince.*

"Stew him in a big ole pot and till Easter, ye'll eat a lot!" the grandpa rhymed with a smile.

Since lunch, they've been workin' at it. Three trains already got stopped in Vagino."

Rebrov looked at his watch.

"22:16. We're seventeen minutes late. Everyone get ready . . ."

Two passengers got on the train at Achinsk: a man in a short sheepskin coat and a kubanka hat carrying a suitcase and a woman with two bags and a white puffy jacket.

"Ogaos," Rebrov said quietly, turning pale.

At 23:51, they passed through Tarutino and Rebrov nodded. Olga pulled her pistol out of her bag and pulled back the slide.

"Everyone onto the floor. The partitions are paper-thin."

"I think they're wearing bulletproof vests," Shtaube mumbled, as he got down.

"Thanks!" Olga laughed nervously, jumped out into the hallway, and shot the worker standing by the window twice. He began to fall and the two other workers jumped out into the hallway with pistols in their hands and opened fire.

"Get down!" the man who had gotten onto the train at Achinsk shouted from behind Olga and she got down onto the ground, still shooting at the workers. The man in the kubanka hat let forth a long burst of fire from an assault rifle and the workers fell to the ground. A policeman with an assault rifle appeared out from the vestibule behind the fallen workers, Olga and the man in the kubanka hat fired, and the policeman fell. A man with a pistol leaned out of compartment no. 8 and shot at the woman in the white puffy jacket, who was holding an assault rifle and standing with her back to the man in the kubanka hat. Letting out a protracted shriek, she responded with a long burst of fire, the man began to sink down in the doorway, his companion began to shoot, using the corpse for cover, but Olga managed to stand up and nail him in the head with two bullets, to which the man in the kubanka hat generously added with his assault rifle. Continuing to shriek, the woman sat down on the floor and let go of the assault rifle.

"Di' they ge' ye, Vasilya?" stepping over her fur boots and speaking in a mix of Russian and Ukrainian, the man in the kubanka hat walked through the car, finishing off the wounded passengers. "Ye hookers! Ye stinkin' maggots!"

Olga jerked open the door to the second compartment, shot a sleeping woman in the face, and ran over to the conductress's compartment: she was sitting on the floor, holding on to her wounded wrist, while a walkie-talkie wheezed next to her. Olga shot the walkie-talkie from across the compartment with her pistol and then pointed it at the conductress.

"How about that tea?"

Having finished off the passengers, the man in the kubanka hat locked the door to the vestibule, then returned to his wounded friend.

"Where'd they ge' ye, Vasilya?"

"Gimme . . ." the woman hiccupped and blood poured from her mouth and onto her white puffy jacket.

Rebrov and Shtaube leaned out of their compartment.

"What are ye bastards doin' hidin' like rats and makin' the lady fight?" the man in the kubanka hat turned to them angrily.

"That's how we do it," muttered Rebrov.

"That's how ye do it? Well, go on, help the lil' one then!" he replaced his clip and walked into the conductress's compartment, in front of which Olga was waiting. "Aha. There she is, our sweet peach, what's a hot pussy like ye doin' in a place like this? How many pigs're left on the train?"

"I dunno," the conductress frowned in pain, "they're all . . . in the first car. I really have nothing to do with it . . ."

"And this doesn't have anything to do with it either?" Olga pointed her gun at the walkie-talkie.

"It's theirs . . ." the conductress sobbed, "they made me. They said they'd kill my mother . . ."

"Don't fuckin' squeal on your people," Olga sneered.

"Mikola . . . Mi . . . kola . . ." the wounded woman wheezed. Rebrov lifted her head.

"What is it Vasilya?" Mikola walked over. "Did the bastards graze ye? It ain't nothin'! We'll git to where we're goin' an' git ye glued back together."

"Mikola . . . tell Staple . . . not to invest my share . . ."

"Ye'll tell 'im that yerself, my darlin'. We two still got a few more tours left in us: fields of flowers to pick and time to dry 'em!"

Blood began to flow from the woman's mouth again and she coughed. Someone whistled in the neighboring vestibule. Olga twitched . . .

"Don't ye worry, it's Marik," Mikola whistled back. Marik appeared in the vestibule wearing the winter uniform of a railwayman and holding a pistol. Having stepped over the policeman's corpse, he raised his assault rifle and looked around.

"What's goin' on here?"

"Everything's right on track. 'Cept they grazed Vaska."

"Is the baggage safe?"

"For now," Rebrov let the now-silent woman's head fall to the floor.

"Root'll put the brakes down next to the forest lane," Marik put his pistol into his pocket.

"Ain't a bad idea," Mikola nodded.

"What about Kozulka?" Rebrov asked.

"They're waitin' for you in Kozulka with gifts," Marik smirked and nodded to Mikola. "Get the cracker ready."

"Ye got it," Mikola said in Ukrainian, dragging two bags filled with cans of gasoline and tolite charges out of the compartment.

"Let's get the baggage," Marik, Rebrov, and Olga took everything out of the compartment and into the vestibule. Mikola began to unwrap the Bickford fuse.

"And who's this?" Marik looked at the conductress.

"A loyal friend to the police," Olga smirked, buttoning her fur coat.

"Mhmm," Marik thought for a second, then tore a piece off of one of the sheets, "well, let's see your wound."

The girl held out her arm and Marik quickly bandaged it up, tying the knot tightly. She let forth a cry.

"Don't be afraid," he wiped her bloodstained hand on the duvet. "And now, the hooves are stirrin'. You're comin' with us. As the pigs' extraordinary and plenipotentiary representative."

"Sir, please don't!" the girl got up onto her knees. "I have a sick mother in Krasnoyarsk and my father is a disabled veteran."

"Be a smarty-pants and you'll see your disabled family again. What d'you have in there?" he kicked at the bag with the pig's head in it.

"A boar's head," the conductress sobbed.

"Where's the tea?"

"Up there."

He opened the cabinet and began to take out packets of tea, sugar, and cookies and put them into the bag with the pig's head.

"It's ready," Mikola said in Ukrainian and showed them the end of the fuse.

"Hold on," Marik dragged the bag into the hallway. "Everyone to the vestibule!"

"Your hat, Seryozha!" Olga pushed the boy, he ran off, then returned with his shapka.

The train began to brake sharply.

"Light the fire when I wave my hand!" Marik opened the door and frosty air burst into the vestibule. "Come on, ladies and gents! The snow's deep here!"

Rebrov was the first to jump with the intermediate block, followed by Olga with the liquid mother, then Seryozha with the knapsack and Shtaube. A lantern flashed three times at the front of the train and Marik responded with a flashlight and waved to Mikola.

"Light it!"

"I damn well am!" Mikola lit the fuse, ran into the vestibule, and gave the conductress a shove with his assault rifle. "C'mon and jump, bitch!"

The conductress jumped and Mikola and Marik jumped after her. The cars of the train jerked and accelerated dangerously. The train disappeared.

"Suck a fuckin' cock!" Shtaube wiped snow from his face and, embedded in a snowdrift, attempted to turn over. "We're here . . ."

It was dark all around. The hazy moon weakly outlined the edge of a forest and low hills in the distance.

"How's the mother?" Rebrov pulled the intermediate block out of the snow and put it down on the almost-invisible crossties.

"Just fine!" Olga picked up the suitcase with some difficulty and cried out, "How're you over there, Seryozha?"

"A-okay!" Seryozha shouted.

Five minutes later, Marik walked over with three assault rifles, accompanied by Mikola, who was carrying the bag, and the weeping, limping conductress. Marik shined his flashlight on them.

"How's the baggage?"

"Everything's fine," Rebrov replied.

"I lost my cane," Shtaube rummaged through the snow. "Shine it over here!"

Marik did so.

"We braked a lil' late. We'll have to stomp our way over to the forest lane."

"Is it far?" Rebrov looked around.

"Less than a kilometer."

"That's fuckin' nothin'!" Shtaube got up from his knee. "At least you give me a hand, Seryozh!"

In the direction in which the train had disappeared, there was a faint, brief flash and the sound of an explosion.

"Oof! Right in the noggin'!" Mikola smiled. "Ours'll shoot up sweeter."

Soon, a bright flash lit up the horizon.

"Oof, that's nice!" Mikola clicked his tongue. "'Cause I was startin' to wonder. Oof! Here's to a long-ass life!" he took off his kubanka hat and prostrated himself to the glow.

"My cane . . . my boxwood cane . . ." Shtaube hadn't stopped looking, "I've had it since '58!"

"We'll find you a new cane," Marik turned off his flashlight. "Let's go, we don't have much time."

Shtaube spat, got up out of the snowdrift, and grabbed Rebrov's attaché case and his own briefcase. Marik took the suitcase with the liquid mother from Olga and Mikola and Rebrov hoisted up the box with the intermediate block. They moved along the snow-covered railroad. Twenty minutes later, they heard a whistle from behind.

"Stop," Marik put down the suitcase and whistled back. Two men wearing railway uniforms caught up with them: one had a Kalashnikov with a truncated barrel hanging from his chest and the other one was carrying a small bag.

"I can't believe it, Marik, I forgot your binoculars back there!" the one with the assault rifle began, smiling and breathing heavily. "When we were dragging that bullshit around, I took 'em off so they wouldn't dangle around, then that putz with the blaster fell down and, basically, while Root and I were givin' him a talkin' to, I just totally and, well . . . totally naturally forgot your binoculars!"

"My binoculars . . ." Marik shook his tired hand. "Well, Kolya *totally naturally* forgot Vasilya too."

"Whaddaya mean? Did she kick it?"

"She croaked, Buttercup," Mikola blew his nose loudly and wiped his hand off on his short sheepskin coat. "Those bastards were dug in like worms in carrion, we couldn't even see where they were firin' from! I'd just managed to sew one 'er two of 'em up when a couple more popped up 'n popped her right in the chest."

"Motherfucker," Root shook his head.

"And I still owed her a couple sniffs I didn't get to give 'er," Buttercup sighed.

"You can give 'em to me," Marik laughed exhaustedly. "And, of course, you didn't pop into the restaurant."

"When would we've had the time, Marik?!"

"Staple's gonna skin us alive."

"The restaurant!" Root grinned spitefully. "It should be enough we got out alive. Let's have a smoke."

Olga opened her cigarette case and held it out. Root, Buttercup, and Mikola each took a cigarette.

"We'll light up when we get into the forest," Marik picked up the suitcase. "Just wait, it's a stone's throw away . . ."

They walked along the railroad for two hundred meters, turned left, and walked through deep snow across a narrow clearing and into the forest. They lit up. Marik whistled. Someone nearby whistled back.

"Oh!" Mikola clicked his tongue. "Nice guess . . ."

They walked a little further.

"Peekaboo!" a man came out from behind a thick pine tree wearing a long fur coat, a big wooly hat, and with a double-barreled rifle over his shoulder. Two horses harnessed to a pair of sleds and barely distinguishable in the darkness were standing next to him.

"You made it!" the man laughed, "And I heard it go up!"

"Yo, Vitya," frowning, Marik put down the suitcase. "Oof, holy fuck . . . that bag is gonna dislocate my shoulder . . ."

"It's not on purpose," Seryozha said.

"Well, how'd it all go? You bring everything?"

"Vasilya kicked it," Marik relit his cigarette.

"The fuck! Were there a lot of cops?"

"A shitload."

"Those weren't cops at all," said Rebrov, breathing heavily.

"Who were they, then?" said Buttercup, turning to face him. "The KGB or something?"

"Not the KGB either."

"Who was it, then?"

"Later, I'll tell you later," Rebrov waved his hand exhaustedly.

"Well, then, let's go," Marik walked over to the horses. The conductress fell to her knees.

"My darlings, my kind friends, please let me go! I didn't do anything to you and I don't know anything! They didn't even tell me who they were or where they were from, they just came in and pulled out their guns! Let me go!"

She began to sob.

"Ye come on over to the sleds, bitch!" Mikola spat at her.

"You're going to kill me! My friends! My darlings! There's no need! I'll bring you money! Let me go and don't kill me! I'm pregnant!"

"You think you're important enough to kill?" Marik smirked, taking the blanket from the horse's back. "We don't kill chicks. We'll fuck you a little, then we'll let you go. We won't touch the baby. Get in 'n stop dillydallying."

The sobbing conductress sat down in a sled. Marik, Olga, Seryozha, and Rebrov sat down next to her with the liquid mother. Having picked up the baggage, the rest of them got into the second, more spacious sled.

"You first, Vit," Marik untangled the frozen reins, gave them a jerk, and the horse pulled the sleds to the left.

"Wh-oa!" Vitya pulled on the horse's reins and the sleds scraped onto a recently paved track. "You hear that? So much snow fell down in the valley that we gotta drive over stone."

"Who gives a damn," Marik wrapped his scarf around the bottom of his face and threw a blanket over his legs, "over the stone we go."

They set off. The track weaved between the trees and, up to their knees in snow, the horses pulled the sleds. The moon came out from behind the clouds and lit up the old, snow-covered coniferous forest.

"Is it a long ride?" Rebrov asked.

"Three hours or so," Marik replied, shifting his scarf. "Once we make it around the taiga, we'll be on a normal road."

For forty minutes, they rode silently behind Vitya's overloaded sled, on which there was continuous and lively conversation. Squished between Olga and Rebrov, the conductress would occasionally cry for a few minutes before falling silent. Further along in the forest, they found themselves in front of a series of posts wrapped in barbed wire.

"What's this? A camp?" Olga asked.

"It says right there," Marik smirked, pulling up his collar.

They drove up closer. A series of identical metal plaques were affixed to the posts:

NO ENTRY!
RADIOACTIVE AREA!
DANGER OF DEATH!

The sleds passed between two poles, the barbed wire connecting which had been cut in half and wrapped around them.

"Is there really danger of death?" Seryozha asked.

"It's not dangerous during the winter," Marik lit up.

"Get your nose out of it!" Rebrov retorted loudly. "Get your snout out of it!"

Seryozha went silent. Olga hugged him, pressed his body to hers, and pulled his hat down over his eyes.

"Go to sleep, my sweet little babe."

"You go to sleep!" Seryozha grumbled.

As they drove down from the hills, they came onto a wide, snow-covered road marked by a sled's barely perceptible tracks.

"Not such a shitty road!" Mikola shouted. "Catch 'em, Marik!"

Vitya whistled, then whipped the horse and it began to trot heavily through the snow. Marik whipped his horse, the sled jerked, and the horse began to gallop. The road ran along the edge of a large hill, next to which was a series of heavily slanted telegraph poles wrapped in torn, tangled wires. The moon shined brightly.

"No cars here?" Olga asked, winking at Rebrov.

"Not for twenty-seven years," Marik replied.

"My hand hurts! I'm gonna die! I need to go to a hospital!" the conductress sobbed.

"Is it still bleeding?" Olga helped her to take her hand out from the bosom of her railway overcoat. The white fabric was almost completely soaked in blood.

"I can't feel it! It's like it's gone numb!" the girl cried.

"Stop whining, we'll be there soon," shivering, Marik spat out his cigarette butt, "our doctor's better than anyone at a hospital."

"Let's tie another scarf around the elbow," Olga took off her scarf and began to tie it around the conductress's arm.

Twice, the road was blocked by deep ditches, which they had to maneuver around by driving into the forest.

"Here we fucking go!" Marik led his horse by its bridle, helping it to get out of the snow. "When we get close to Kozulka, there'll be so much snow it'll be impossible to even walk. Two layers of barbed wire . . ."

They rode for another twenty-five kilometers, the road passed around a steep hill and slid down into a wide valley, almost the entire space of which was occupied by an abandoned city.

"Come on, Lena, watch your pissing knees!" cried Vitya, pulling on the horse's reins. The sleds sped down the hill. Mikola whistled. Marik whipped his horse as he hurried past Vitya's sled. They passed by a mass of rusty, snow-covered machinery, went around the decrepit Sayany Cinema, overgrown with fir trees, and rode along Chekhov Street. On both sides of the street, there were rows of three-story brick houses with broken windows and collapsed roofs. A store building was filled with trees and bushes; a cedar tree was growing through the roof of a bus outside of it. They turned left and drove along a wide street.

"What was this city called?" asked Seryozha.

"Like the river. Chulym," Marik removed his scarf from his face. "We're lucky, ladies and gents, to have such a fair wind. If it'd been coming off of the hills, that would've been fucked up. Staple would've had to pry us out of the sleds with a crowbar."

They approached the five-story building of the city party committee and Mikola whistled. The oaken gates of the main entrance opened and a man wearing a coat and hat and holding a double-barreled rifle came through the opening.

"Hello, hello, and he froze. Like matches."

Not paying any attention to him, Vitya and Marik jumped out of the sled, grabbed the horses by their bridles, and led them into the vestibule of the city committee.

"That's how they did it out there," the man in the hat grinned, pulling the bolt on the door shut, "hello, hello, and enough."

Two kerosene lamps were burning in the freezing vestibule. They got out of the sleds and began to collect their baggage.

"Did you warm the water?" Marik asked the man in the hat.

"I warmed up the water, warmed up the water, warmed up the water," he began to unharness the horse.

"Oy! I can't straighten my back!" Vitya stretched out.

"What's this?" Seryozha walked over to the watchman's table, on which there was a dead hare the size of a pig. The hare's hunchback was covered with knobbly growths and its mouth, dark with blood, snarled opened to reveal its yellow front teeth.

"The gifts of nature. A saber-tooth hare," Marik coughed, picking up the bag. "Don't overfeed him, Tolyap."

"Feed, feed, and still—hello," the man in the hat led a horse behind a clothing rack and put a bucket of water in front of it.

"The znedo doesn't come first," Rebrov hissed at Olga.

"Sterile! To me too!" Olga snorted at him.

They took the baggage and went down into the basement. Marik pointed his flashlight at a steel door and knocked.

"Who is it?" someone behind the door said weakly.

"Baldokh!" Marik shouted.

The massive door opened, breathing warmth and light.

"How perfect!" Weakling laughed, letting down the barrel of his rifle and moving over to the side. "Buncha fuckin' iceboaters . . ."

"You old club, you! You jumping frog!" Buttercup breathed into his face.

"I saw a birch tree, Weakling," Vitya winked at him, carrying the suitcase with the liquid mother.

"Oh, I'm afraid we *all* saw that there birch!" Mikola laughed.

"Iceboaters! Iceboaters!" Weakling smiled, locking the door.

The basement was heated to the point of stuffiness, the matte ceiling lights shined forth with an even light, and the walls were paneled with polished wood. They began to take off their winter layers in a small cloakroom.

"My God, can it really be this warm?" Shtaube unwound his scarf. "Is the shitter heated too?"

"Of course," Marik removed his tight railwayman jacket. "For as long as we've got enough diesel, no question."

Olga helped the pale, unsteady conductress to undress.

"Clomp, clomp, to the boss," Weakling nodded.

Walking along the blue carpet, they moved down the hallway. All of the denizens of the basement had the crowns of their heads neatly shaved.

"Clomp," Weakling stopped outside of a door with a plaque reading "2nd Secretary," and knocked.

"Go rob!" someone cried out from behind the door.

"Suck my dick!" Marik exchanged a look with Weakling. "Has he . . . already?"

"A man can't carry another man on a board," Weakling laughed and opened the door.

They walked into a spacious office filled to the brim with all sorts of odds and ends. Staple was sitting naked on a mattress in the corner of the room and watching a video. There was a PKC machine gun with an ammunition belt lying next to him on the bed. Staple's head was shaved and there was a round bandage on its crown. He didn't look away from the television, on which *Casablanca* was playing.

"Clomp, clomp, anybody home?" said Weakling.

"Go rob!" Staple shouted so loudly and so protractedly that his sweaty, tattooed body shook.

"We brought guests with us, Mish," Marik said cautiously.

"Go ro-o-ob!" Staple shouted.

"Pukhnachyov and Menzelintsev," Rebrov pronounced loudly.

"Go ro-o-ob!"

"Designs by secondary mechanical engineers, project no. 365," Rebrov continued.

"Go ro-o-ob! Go ro-o-ob! Go ro-o-ob!" Staple jumped up and pointed the machine gun at Rebrov. Marik pushed Rebrov off to the side, then grabbed Mikola by the hair and threw him into the opposite corner of the study.

"Grey!"

"Go ro-o-o-o-ob!!!" Staple squeezed the trigger. Large-caliber bullets shredded Mikola's body.

"Look, if you'd just touch the wire for my . . ." a calm voice came through an intercom on a cluttered desk.

"Go rob?" Staple dropped the machine gun and sniffed at his fingers.

The conductress's legs buckled and she fell to the floor.

"Who was it, Marik?" the voice coming through the intercom asked.

"Mikolka, Doc," Marik took a dry piece of bread off of the intercom and dropped it on the ground, "he double-crossed Vasilya."

"Go ro-o-ob!" Staple roared.

"I've always said that Ukrainians are fuckin' unreliable people," the voice continued. "How much money?"

There was a PKC machine gun with an ammunition belt lying next to him on the bed.

"Two thou, Doc."

"Congratulations," the voice laughed. "And to eat?"

"Yeah, a lil' bit of that too," Marik sighed, "and we have a girl here who's, uh, entirely fuckable, Doc. She just passed out for a sec."

"I understand," the voice yawned. "Okay, pass through one by one. And Susanin needs to march, march, march right to the kitchen."

Root picked up the bag and, muttering unhappily, walked out.

"Go rob! Rob! Rob!" Staple shouted.

"Pukhnachyov and Menzelintsev!" Rebrov walked over to the desk and leaned down toward the intercom. "Pukhnachyov and Menzelintsev!"

"We already heard you, why the shouting?" someone answered and the intercom went silent.

"Mish, tell Tolyapa to drag this faggot upstairs," Marik nodded at the corpse swimming in its own blood.

"Go rob!" Staple cried out sharply, jumping up onto the mattress.

They went out into the hallway. Walked for a little while, then stopped outside of a door with a plaque reading, "1st Secretary."

"The first honeybear," Weakling stroked the crown of Marik's head, "jump, jump!"

Marik walked in and Weakling shut the door behind him.

"The second honeybear'll feel as if t'were at home with Mommy. Spray it."

Vitya walked in next.

"The third fart'll waft up and that'll be that!" Weakling laughed, exposing his broken teeth.

"I'm ready to let one fuckin' rip, Weakling," Buttercup muttered excitedly as he walked in.

"And then it'll be time for candy bars," Weakling laughed, going through the door behind Buttercup.

"What're you doing?!" Shtaube hissed palely at Rebrov.

"Vitya, Vitya!" Olga squeezed his hand. "Maybe they don't know anything! Why should we wait around? Build a bridge, baby!"

"Don't interfere," Rebrov pulled his hand free and opened the door. They walked into a tidy, spacious office. Doc was sitting at his desk. Weakling was on his knees next to the armchair, muttering something and grabbing at Doc's knees.

"Hands, hands," Doc slapped Weakling's hand, rubbed the shaved crown of his head with alcohol, waited for a minute, then rubbed it with a greenish fluid.

"Oh, my darling birdy, oh my darling . . ." Weakling muttered, trembling.

Standing next to him, Kolya grabbed on to Weakling's head delicately. Doc put his rubber-gloved hand into a ten-liter glass jar, rummaged through rotten leaves, and pulled out a fat bluish-grey slug.

"Birdy, birdy, birdy!" Weakling began to tremble. Doc put the slug on the crown of his head. Kolya brought Weakling, now sobbing, up off of his knees, and led him over to a long table, at which Marik, Buttercup, and Vitya were sitting motionlessly. Slugs were stirring very slightly on the crowns of their heads. Doc sat Weakling down next to Vitya.

"Start out on the fours," Doc said, taking off his glove. Kolya took out two meter-long spokes from a battered tube and rubbed them with alcohol. The men sitting at the table raised their left palms. Having pierced them one by one through the *he-gu* point, he skewered all of their hands on the first meter-long spoke. The men sitting at the table then raised their right palms. Kolya skewered them with the second spoke.

"Give 'em thirty so they don't get all whiny afterward," Doc bound the mouth of the jar with a roll of gauze.

Kolya turned on the rheostat, adjusted it, and connected its terminals to the ends of the spokes. The men sitting at the table began to shake. The slugs on their heads turned pink. When they'd turned the color of ripe cherries, Kolya turned off the rheostat. The men collapsed

He skewered all of their hands on the first meter-long spoke.

face-first onto the table. Kolya put on his rubber glove, took the slugs off of the men's heads, put them into the blue glass jar, then closed its lid. Meanwhile, Doc cut four circles out of capsicum bandages and walked over to the men. Kolya wiped the crowns of their heads with alcohol and Doc stuck the round bandages onto them. While Kolya was removing the spokes from their palms, Doc took a cone-shaped felt suitcase locked with a miniature padlock out of a safe. After undoing the lock, he opened the suitcase and took out a narrow golden pyramid, the tip of which was made out of silvery-green metal. Then, having sucked transparent liquid from a vial and into a syringe, Doc roughly stuck the needle into the tip of the pyramid and injected it.

"Come on, y'round-bottomed dolls . . ." Kolya began to slap the men on their cheeks. "Le-e-esss go! No time to waste."

They gradually came to their senses.

"Quickly! Quickly!" Doc banged his palms against the table. "Who's gonna to suck the wedge?"

"I will," Weakling whispered.

"I will," Buttercup whispered.

"And the friction?"

"Me," Vitya whispered.

"Me," Marik whispered.

Doc handed the pyramid to Weakling, who immediately began to suck its peak. Kolya handed Vitya and Marik two identical ebonite sticks. Facing each other, Vitya and Marik got down onto their knees, put their foreheads together, and began to quickly rub each other's necks with the sticks.

"Can I be on white today, Doc?" Kolya asked.

"Hold on, you're gonna help with the chick now," Doc put away the syringe and the vial.

"In the joinery again?" Kolya asked sadly.

"Yeah, yeah," Doc walked out into the hallway.

"Listen! Can you finally give us just a moment of your attention?" Rebrov walked after him.

"Yeah, yeah, let's go now . . ." Doc walked down the hallway, unlocked the door to the joinery, walked in, and turned on the light. Rebrov, Shtaube, Olga, and Seryozha walked in after him. Kolya brought in the staggering conductress and began to quickly undress her.

"Just a sec, just a sec . . ." Doc nodded reassuringly at Rebrov, picked up a belt, and tied the girl's bare elbows together behind her back. The girl screamed.

"Don't be afraid, it's not gonna hurt," Kolya unbuttoned her black skirt.

"I'm pregnant," the girl wept.

"Wow, yeah . . . I see . . . the tummy . . ." Kolya tugged at her skirt.

"Guys! My mother's sick and my father's disabled. Will you let me go?"

"We'll let you go," Doc nodded, rummaging through the instruments.

"Your . . . the other guy said you'd fuck me a little, then let me go, but you wouldn't touch the baby . . . I can give you money, guys!" she sobbed.

"We'll fuck you a little, then let you go. That's exactly right. We won't touch the baby. I can guarantee that. Come on now," Doc walked over to a carpentry bench.

Kolya dragged the naked girl over and they quickly clamped her head in a wooden vice. She screamed loudly.

"Come on, don't be scared, it really won't hurt," Kolya loosened the clamp slightly. Doc brought an electric planer to the back of the girl's head and turned it on. The girl shrieked. Bone shavings fell to the floor.

"Enough, enough," he turned off the planer, examined the hole in the back of the girl's head, then began to unbutton his pants. The girl shrieked and blood flowed down her back in a delicate stream.

Doc pulled down his pants, pulled off his underwear, and put his erect penis into the hole.

"Sweetie . . ."

His penis went into the girl's skull, squeezing out part of her brain. The girl began to low and her bare feet knocked against the floor.

"Sweetie, sweetie, sweetie," Doc moved rhythmically and leaned against the bench.

The girl lowed. Blood and brain matter oozed down her back. Her legs twitched convulsively, blood flowed from her vagina, and she passed gas.

"Sweetie, sweetie, swe-e-e-eti-i-i-ie," Doc moaned, putting his face to the bench.

"Now we're really fuckin'," Kolya smiled as he rummaged through the instruments.

Doc moaned loudly and froze. The girl twitched silently. Doc rose back up and his penis left the girl's skull with a smack. He walked over to a stool with a pan on it. Kolya gave him a bit of soap and poured water sparingly from a bottle.

"Oy, oy . . ." Doc sighed, leisurely washing his penis.

"Bird's nest!" Kolya laughed.

"Pukhnachyov and Menzelintsev!" Rebrov yelled, having lost his patience. "Pukh-na-chyov! Men-ze-lin-tsev!"

"How many times have you said that now?" Doc chuckled.

"I wonder who you think we are, kind friend? Your poor relatives?!" Shtaube twitched. "Beggars?! I could be your father!"

"We've already lost an hour!"

"You're gonna have to wait till dawn in any case," Doc wiped off his penis with the towel Kolya handed to him. "You can't go into the hangars at night."

"What if we've got lanterns?" Rebrov asked.

"You'll break your necks. Everything's in a terrible state, it's all falling apart."

"Then why . . . why the fuck were we in such a rush?!" Shtaube exclaimed.

"Please don't speak like that in my presence," Doc frowned and buttoned up his pants. "Do you have the chest?"

"We do."

"Show me."

Rebrov opened the attaché case, pulled out the bag with a piece of Leontiev's chest in it, and handed it to Doc. Doc untied the bag and looked inside.

"So. Scar, hairs, nipple. On New Year's, I personally kissed 'em . . . Kol, take this upstairs with the chick."

He dropped the bag onto the ground. Kolya undid the vice atop the bench and the corpse tumbled to the ground.

"Just a lil' while longer and she would've had the kid!" Kolya winked at Olga and pulled the corpse's legs apart. A baby's little head was peeking out from the corpse's genitals.

"Where's the intermediate block?" Doc walked out into the hallway.

"Over there," Rebrov followed him out. Marik and Vitya were crawling around outside Staple's room. Tolyapa's sobs came through the open door.

"Over here," Doc lifted up the intermediate block, walked into the communications room, and set the box on a table. "Oy, what a monster . . ."

"Ouchie . . . ou-u-uchie . . ." Tolyapa cried.

"Open it," Doc unlocked a fireproof cabinet.

Rebrov opened the intermediate block. Marik and Vitya crawled in through the door. Doc took the blit and the cartridge out of the cabinet and began to screw them together.

"My God," mumbled Shtaube, "and I thought . . . my God!"

Rebrov turned the transverse-supply lever, moved the gnek to 3 and the pole to 2. Marik kissed Doc's boot.

"Go away," Doc kicked him.

"Ouchiii-agghhhh! Ouchiii-agghhhhh!" Tolyapa screamed.

"Lock the door," Doc mumbled, walking over and leaning down to the intermediate block.

Olga locked the door. Doc put the blit onto the axial next and began to turn it cautiously. Rebrov pushed the transverse-supply lever. The gnek turned and the blit began to plunge into the nest.

"All without any electronics," Doc chuckled, "just don't force it."

"Of course!" Rebrov muttered happily. "6, then 8, then on to the paraclete."

Marik crawled over to Doc and kissed his boot. Rebrov turned the feed to 6.

"Go rob! Go rob!" Staple knocked on the door.

The blit plunged down to the red risk. Rebrov turned the feed to 8 and pulled on the paraclete.

"Go rob! Go rob!" Staple knocked.

"Bastard . . . I'll make you chop wood tomorrow!" Doc shouted.

Marik crawled over to Olga's feet. The blit sank down to the main mark. Rebrov turned off the feed, turned the znedo to 0, and sighed with relief.

"Hup."

Olga reached for her bag, but Marik grabbed her by the legs and yanked. She fell. Vitya grabbed the bag.

"Nobody move," Doc snatched a pistol from his pocket, pointed it at Rebrov, backed away toward the door, and unlocked it. The remaining denizens of the basement burst into the room with weapons in hand.

"Gah! Cunt! The bitch's really thrashin'!" Marik struggled with Olga, twisting back her arm.

"Hands behind your heads!" Tolyapa commanded and knocked Rebrov off of his feet with a lightning-fast blow.

Shtaube and Seryozha put their hands up.

"Woah," Vitya pulled the pistol out of Olga's bag and handed it to Tolyapa. Without looking, Tolyapa stuck the pistol into his waistband, gave Shtaube a shove, and walked over to the intermediate block.

"Well?"

"Everything's done, absolutely everything," Doc waved his hands. "Kill the motherfuckers dead."

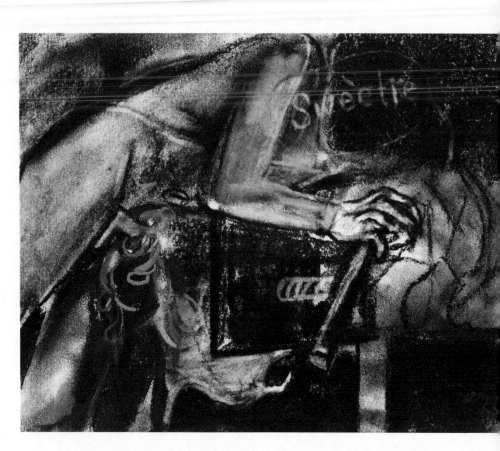

"Sweetie, sweetie, sweetie," Doc moved rhythmically and leaned against the bench.

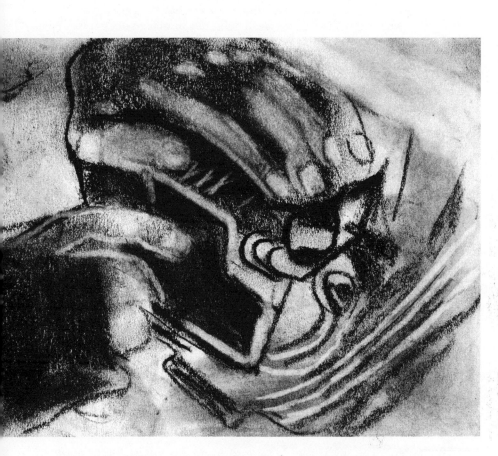

Rebrov turned the transverse-supply lever, moved the gnek to 3 and the pole to 2.

"And the lock?

"What about the lock? We'll open the lock ourselves."

" *You* will?"

"Well . . . we'll all do it. We'll definitely be able to open it."

"We'll be able to open it? Oh brother . . ." Tolyapa shook his head surprisedly and kicked Doc in the chest. Doc flew onto the ground.

"The brat knows all about the lock, Gen," Staple said, "Leontiev pointed at 'im."

"You and Leontiev can go get ass-fucked," Tolyapa closed the intermediate block.

Marik bent back Olga's arm and sat on her legs.

"There you go, bitch."

Tolyapa grabbed Seryozha by the hair.

"Well? How about that lock?"

"Suck my dick! Suck my dick!" Seryozha yelled, breaking free from his arms.

Tolyapa threw Seryozha down onto the ground.

"I won't just suck your dick. I'll suck your balls, your eyes, your ears, I'm gonna suck every part of you until you tell us the combination. Take him to the shower. And frisk these guys. Then to the aircon. Fish, Valtik, you're in charge of 'em."

Weakling and Buttercup dragged Seryozha away.

"If your little faggot doesn't tell us the combo, we'll tear all your guts out," Tolyapa kicked Olga with his boot. "And I'll tear out your cunt. Personally."

They searched Rebrov, Olga, and Shtaube, then pushed them into a dark, empty pantry. Vitya locked the door. Root dragged a bench over and pushed it against the door. They sat down on the bench.

"He broke something," Rebrov touched his body in the darkness, "oy, it hurts . . ."

"To shit the bed like that!" Shtaube exhaled. "To shit and piss everything away in a single instant! What happened to your reflexes, Olga Vladimirovna?"

"And where were you . . . bastards! bastards! bastards! Vitya! How can it be like this?! How did they know? Vitya! Vitya!"

Rebrov was silent. The sound of Seryozha's heartrending cry reached the cellar.

"Bastards! Bastards!" Olga hammered at the door. "You fucking pigs! Let him go!"

"We'll let him go," someone said from behind the door. "We'll gut him, then we'll let him go."

"You fucking asshole! You piece of shit!"

"If you keep on yappin' like that, I'll throw you out into the cold."

Seryozha screamed.

"Bastards! What're they gonna do to him? Vitya! How can you just sit there!" she pushed him in the dark.

"Agh!" Rebrov cried out. "That hurts . . . It was probably Golubyov. Yeah. I didn't check the allotment of his series. He could've known Leontiev. 62, 1. That's not kleno, that's, hold on . . . No!" he slid over to the door. "Hold on! Open up! You can't touch him! You can't destroy him!"

"You've done it now, really done it! Puh! Suck a fuckin' dick!" Shtaube spat. "You're up to your mouths in shit! Your mouths! Breathe deep, assholes!"

"Seryozhenka . . . bastards! He doesn't know anything! You stupid fucks! You're gonna ruin everything! Open up, you pig!"

"I'll open you up," Vitya replied as he chewed.

"Fuck you! All of you . . ." Shtaube rolled up his pant leg and began to unfasten his prosthesis in the dark. "Time to blow the fuck up. That's enough!"

"What d'you mean? How?" Rebrov asked distractedly.

"I've got a grenade in my prosthesis. Let's end it in one go. I don't have any strength left . . . fuck the fundaments . . ."

"What kind of grenade?" Olga touched the old man's sweaty head.

"A normal one . . . Fuck knows what kind, darling, come on . . . It'll kill us all the same, Olenka . . ."

"Hold on . . . where?"

"Here, at the base, pull out the wire and there's a string in the tube . . . Come on, darlings, put your heads onto the prosthesis and I'll pull the string."

"Come on, give it here," Olga took the prosthesis from Shtaube and whispered, "What weapons do they have outside?"

"One has a pistol, the other has . . . I can't remember, Olenka, baby, they're gonna rip your cunt out and fuck us all in the brain! Let's just blow ourselves up!"

"Quiet, don't yell. Crawl into the far corner, Vitya, go over there quick. Block up your ears and open your mouths."

"Olya! Olya!"

"Crawl! I'm not gonna wait!" she placed the prosthesis on the door handle and knocked at the door. "Hey, guys! I have a real important message for you!"

"We're listening, Comrade Cunt!" Vitya laughed.

Olga pulled out the wire, jerked the string, and threw herself into the corner.

The explosion blew the door off of its hinges. Olga ran out into the smoky hallway and grabbed the Makarov pistol out of Vitya's pocket. His body had been torn apart. At the opposite end of the hallway, Marik, Weakling, and Kolya ran out of the shower room. Getting down onto her knees, Olga opened fire. Marik fell and Weakling and Kolya fired back with their assault rifles. Olga rushed into the cellar across the hallway. Rebrov grabbed Root's twitching, bloody leg and pulled him into the first cellar. Shtaube pulled a Nagant revolver out of Root's waistband and began to shoot, leaning out through the blown-out door. A burst of automatic fire ripped through the doorframe above his head. Shtaube ducked back inside.

"Throw it to me! Don't waste ammo!" Olga yelled. Shtaube threw her the Nagant revolver. "Run to the staircase!" Olga shot four bullets from the revolver, one of which hit Kolya in the chest. Shtaube jumped out into the hallway, his empty pant leg waving around. Rebrov rushed after him with a limp. Tolyapa let forth a long burst of fire, two bullets hit Rebrov in his right side, and Shtaube's index finger flew off of his left hand. Olga dropped the empty Nagant revolver and began to shoot with her pistol. A bullet tore through Tolyapa's cheek.

"Waste 'em! Waste 'em! Waste 'em!" he yelled, taking cover in one of the rooms. Staple appeared in the hallway with a machine gun. Olga ran out the door, through the hallway, and up the stairs. Shtaube pulled Rebrov by the arm.

"C'mon, c'mon!"

Olga grabbed Rebrov by his other arm and they dragged him upstairs.

"The intermediate block . . . we have to turn it to 19 . . ." Rebrov coughed.

"Your intermediate block can get fucked in the mouth! They're gonna make a sieve out of us!"

"Hide by the horse, it's dark down there! They'll all follow me upstairs and you go down to the basement!" Olga ran up to the second floor. Shtaube and Rebrov disappeared into the vestibule. Staple was the first to run out of the basement and up the stairs, letting forth a long burst of fire.

"Suck a cock, you pig!" Olga shouted from upstairs.

Staple, Weakling, and Buttercup fired back. Pieces of marble and plaster flew down.

"Stop blowin' milk bubbles and get up there!" Tolyapa shouted. Staple, Weakling, and Buttercup ran upstairs.

"Go to the canteen and stand next to the staircase," Tolyapa ordered Doc. Doc ran out of the vestibule and to the right. Tolyapa tore a piece of fabric from his shirt and pressed it to his cheek.

"Motherfuck . . ."

He picked up the assault rifle with his left hand and walked along the left side of the hallway. Olga ran up to the fourth floor, flew down a hallway, and got behind a column in a vestibule. It was cold, but not dark; the moon shined through the vestibule's large, half-broken windows. Olga pulled out her clip and counted how many bullets were left: two in the clip and one in the barrel. She took aim at the corners of one of the windows and whispered, "Bam! Bam! Bam!"

Something rustled on the staircase. Olga took off her boots and held them in her left hand. Weakling moved cautiously along the wall of the hallway, holding his assault rifle at the ready. When he reached the first door, he kicked it open, ran in, looked around, then immediately ran out. As he approached the vestibule, Olga let forth a loud, throaty sound and threw her boots to the left. Weakling fired in the direction of the fallen boots and Olga jumped out from behind the column to the right and fired. The bullet hit Weakling in the left shoulder and he screamed and pulled the trigger of his rifle. Olga jumped twice, very quickly, and fired. The bullet entered Weakling's left side, he screamed and pointed the barrel of his rifle at Olga, she jumped behind the column, and bullets destroyed its marble cladding. Weakling fell to his knees, then jumped back up, made a run for it, fell behind another column, and hoarsely cried out, "Vasya! The loaf!"

Olga let forth another guttural sound and ran out from behind the column. Weakling fired, Olga jumped to the right, to the left, and to the right, then ran over to his column and hid behind it. Weakling folded his legs under him and got up onto his knees. Olga let forth a piercing scream and peered out from the left side of the column, he fired, she jumped to the left, bent over, reached out, and shot him in the face. Footsteps came up the stairs. Olga dropped the pistol, picked up the automatic rifle, ran down the hallway, and jumped through an open door. Staple and Buttercup walked up to the body. Staple squatted down and turned the corpse's mutilated face toward the light.

"Let's look through the offices, I'll cover you."

Buttercup began to inspect the rooms one by one. When he peered into the library, Olga screamed. Buttercup fired a round at the shelves of books. Standing behind one of them, Olga squeezed the trigger of her gun: a long round of fire passed across another shelf, Buttercup, and a window in the vestibule. Olga ran into the depths of the library. Staple ran past Buttercup's twitching body and opened fire with his machine gun. Olga threw herself to the floor. Staple walked down the aisle between the shelves, letting forth short bursts of fire. Large-caliber bullets shredded the books and his ammunition belt dragged along the floor. Lying behind fallen shelves, Olga grabbed a book covered in a thick dust and threw it down the aisle. Staple froze and crouched down. Olga picked up another book and threw it further away. Staple took a book off of the shelf and threw it. Olga picked up a book, sat down, and pointed the assault rifle down the aisle. Staple began to pick up various books and throw them forward. One of them hit Olga. Olga threw her book. Staple sprayed the room with a long round of fire, then listened carefully. Olga puckered her lips and made a soft, delicate sound. Staple moved down the aisle. His ammunition belt scraped across the floor. Olga fell silent. Staple stopped. There was only one bookshelf between them.

"You know," she said.

Staple walked over to her from the aisle and raised his machine gun.

"Come on then."

Olga dropped the assault rifle and stood up.

"It's them."

"And you thought it'd be us?" Staple laughed spitefully. "You shit-ass platochnitsa! Now clomp on over here!"

Olga walked down the aisle and toward the door.

"Can I put on my boots? I didn't . . . recognize you right away . . . you got so fat . . ."

"March!" he shoved her with the barrel of his machine gun. They walked out into the vestibule, then Olga found her boots and began to put them on.

"Did you think up that stuff about Sashka on your own or did your dumbass associates tell you?"

Olga was silent.

Staple walked down the aisle between the shelves, letting forth short bursts of fire.

"You trot along first."

She started to walk down the hallway, blowing on her frigid hands. She stopped short of the back staircase.

"Clomp on down," Staple gave her a shove.

Olga got down onto her knees.

"Hold on . . ."

"What!"

"Hold on . . . I can't do this. Hold on! There's layered paint! I couldn't've come up with everything! You can't do this right now!"

"Go downstairs!" Staple pushed her with his foot. "And keep singin' about the scale!"

"I can't do it right now!" Olga sobbed. "There're markings! I'm not a machine! I love you! I've always loved you! Always, Borya!"

"Go down and stop wastin' time!"

Olga began to walk down the dark staircase. Staple followed her.

"There're markings! I can't! I can't!" she sobbed.

Barely had they gotten past the third floor when a round of automatic fire rang out behind them.

"Get down!"

Bullets knocked plaster from the ceiling. Olga fell to the ground.

"Ours," Staple turned to Tolyapa and let forth a round of fire. Tolyapa tumbled over the bannister and down onto the stairs.

Olga's pistol flew out from his waistband and tumbled down the staircase.

"There's another one!" Olga shouted.

Staple looked up. Olga jumped up and over the banister.

"Sit down!" Staple opened fire.

Olga jumped onto the landing, picked up her pistol, then ran downstairs. A round of automatic fire sounded below and bullets whistled past Olga. She bolted around the corner.

"Sit down, cunt! Sit down, platochnitsa!" Staple walked down the stairs, firing continuously. Olga released the pistol's safety. A round of fire rang out downstairs and bullets flew into the wall next to her. Staple froze. Shell casings bounced down the stairs. A whistle came from downstairs. Staple whistled back. Tolyapa's blood dripped down from the third floor, freezing as it flowed. Tiny pieces of ice spun through the darkness around Olga's legs. Olga jumped to the right, fell to the ground, and rolled into the hallway. People were shooting both above and below her. She jumped up and rushed down the hallway.

"I'm gonna waste you, whore! Sit down!" Staple shouted.

Having run to the end of the hallway, Olga threw open the door in front of her and entered a large room used for committee meetings. The glass in the wide windows was broken and snow covered rows of moldering chairs. Slowed by drifts that reached up to her knees, Olga ran across the room, jumped up onto a dais, leaped over a fallen table covered with shreds of decaying red cloth, and got behind a massive marble bust of Lenin. Staple ran in and sprayed bullets through the room. Olga shot over Lenin's shoulder twice: the first bullet ricocheted off of Staple's machine gun and the second hit him in his right hip. He cried out, threw himself into a snowdrift, rose back up, then opened fire. Chips of marble flew forth from the bust, Olga got down on the ground, crawled over to a ruined piano, and began to take aim, but, right in front of her, a huge, knobby rat with a short if also unusually fat tail appeared out of the piano's wreckage, jumped down heavily from the dais, then ran away unhurriedly. Olga jumped up and, screaming, shot at the rat until her pistol clicked emptily.

"Thanks for that," Doc's voice resounded behind her, "one less pest."

Olga turned around. Doc came out of a hole in the wall at the edge of the room and pointed an assault rifle at her.

"We're on the same side, Vas!"

"I'll waste you, whore! I'll waste you, cunt!" Staple got up out of the snowdrift and limped over to the dais.

"Don't do it, Vitya!" Olga screamed, looking at Doc's back with horror. Doc looked around, Olga jumped over to him, grabbed his assault rifle by the barrel, pushed it up into the air, and a round of fire flew into the ceiling. Olga grabbed on to Doc's face with her other hand and they fell down.

"To me! The whore to me!" Staple limped over to the dais, threw down the machine gun, and climbed on top of Doc and Olga. Doc punched Olga in the head, but let go of the rifle, and Olga tore over to it. Staple grabbed her by the leg, yanked her toward him, and she slid along the frozen, swollen floorboards. Staple pinned her down and bit into her cheek, she screamed, felt for the trigger, and shot Staple in the elbow; his arm flew into the hall, he screamed, a piece of Olga's cheek fell from his mouth, Olga broke away, Doc kicked her in the face, and she flew into the bust of Lenin, dropping the rifle, which Doc then made a run for.

"Cu-u-u-u-unt!" Staple grabbed the machine gun by its barrel and began to swing it around, but Shtaube shot him three times with a pistol. Staple fell from the dais with a scream, Doc rushed toward the bust, Olga grabbed him, Shtaube jumped toward the bust, Doc fired, the round tore through Shtaube's sweater below the armpit, Shtaube fired as he fell and caught Doc in the shoulder with a bullet. Olga grabbed him by the mouth and pulled him down, Doc fell and hit her with the assault rifle, Shtaube crawled over to the bust, fired, and a bullet ripped off Doc's chin and grazed Olga's arm, Shtaube grabbed Doc's head and began to smash it against the corner of the bust.

"Don't breathe! Don't breathe! Don't breathe!"

Olga grabbed the assault rifle, pushed Shtaube away, shot Doc in the face, and blood and brain matter exploded out onto the bust.

"Viktor's barely breathing over there," Shtaube dropped the empty pistol, stood up, and leaned against the bust.

"And Seryozha . . . ?"

"He's alive, gotta unhook him, let's go."

They got down from the dais. Staple was lying next to it in agonizing pain.

"That's my husband . . ." Olga mumbled, clutching her bitten cheek. "He's the one who called Radchenko . . ."

"Boris?" Shtaube moaned.

"Yeah. But I . . . can't kill him . . . I asked Fedenka to do it . . ."

They got up and moved down the aisle, clutching on to each other. Shtaube collapsed.

"Motherfucked . . . keep walking Olenka, I'll crawl."

Olga hung the assault rifle around her neck, picked up a handful of snow, and pressed it to her cheek.

"Get on my back."

"No way, no need . . ."

"Get on my back, c'mon! C'mon!" she shouted. Shtaube got up, wrapped his arms around her neck, and she began walking. They walked through the door and into the hallway. They startled two giant rats eating the conductress's corpse in the vestibule, then walked down into the basement. Seryozha was completely naked and in the shower hanging from a hook stuck into the skin beneath his collarbone. Rebrov was sitting in the corner, applying pressure to his wounds.

"I'll hold 'im . . ." Shtaube grabbed on to Seryozha's legs. Olga shot the rope and Seryozha fell into Shtaube's arms.

"Seryozhenka," Olga pulled the hook and Seryozha moaned.

"My head's . . . swimming," Rebrov closed his eyes palely and shook his head. "A minor allotment . . . quickly . . ."

Olga brought in the suitcase, pulled out the scan, and spread it out on the floor, Shtaube gave Rebrov the ebonite sphere, and Rebrov released it from his bloody fingers. The sphere stopped at "service." Olga put one plate onto 3 and the other onto 7. Shtaube touched the red with the rod. Olga dragged Seryozha over to the scan and began to slap him across the face.

"Seryozhenka, the allotment, Seryozhenka . . ."

Seryozha opened his eyes. Blood flowed from the wound beneath his collarbone in a delicate stream. Olga put a piece of chalk into his hand, then he brought it through "wall-bolt" and dropped it. Rebrov moved the segment to "big" and touched the sphere. The sphere showed "trust." Olga placed the right plate on 29. Shtaube moved through the red with the ring. Olga put the chalk into Seryozha's hand. Seryozha marked "wall-house." Rebrov jabbed his finger at "ned-root," moved the segment to "suppression," and touched the sphere. The sphere showed "pause." Olga moved the left plate to 2. Shtaube touched the yellow with the rod. Seryozha lost consciousness. Olga shook him.

"Seryozh! It's the last circle."

Shtaube slapped his already tortured buttocks.

"Don't let us down, we're almost done."

"I feel . . . so bad. Hurry . . ." Rebrov lay down on his back.

Olga began to hit Seryozha in the face.

"C'mon! C'mon! C'mon!"

"Wake him . . . up," Rebrov sighed heavily, then coughed.

Olga turned on the shower and dragged Seryozha into it. Cold water flowed over his face, Shtaube shook his legs, smearing them with the blood flowing from his finger-stump.

"Wake up, little darling! Wake up for Christ's sake!"

Seryozha didn't budge. Shtaube bit him on the leg and Olga hit him in the face, splashing water everywhere.

"The hook . . ." Rebrov said, looking up at the ceiling.

"Mhmm . . ." Olga let go of Seryozha and bound together the rope she'd shot apart with a marine knot, Shtaube put the hook back into the wound under Seryozha's collarbone, and Olga pulled the rope.

"Please, Seryozhenka, darling!"

Seryozha was suspended above the ground. Shtaube grabbed him by his testicles.

"Wake up, you little prick!"

Seryozha moaned, Olga lowered him down, dragged him over to the scan, and Shtaube placed the chalk into the palm of his hand.

"I'm begging you, Seryozha," Rebrov said, rising up.

Seryozha was completely naked and in the shower hanging from a hook stuck into the skin beneath his collarbone.

Seryozha squeezed the chalk.

"My back . . . hurts . . ."

Olga turned his wet head toward the scan. Still holding the chalk, Seryozha let his hand fall onto "wall-exit." Rebrov pulled on the 7, moved the segment into the field, and touched the sphere. The sphere showed "hop."

Shtaube crossed himself and tossed the rod off to the side. Olga yanked the hook out from under Seryozha's collarbone. Rebrov stood up and leaned against the wall.

"Henry Ivanych . . . find a crowbar . . . or a chisel."

Shtaube jumped out into the hallway. Olga gathered up Seryozha's clothes and put his sweater on.

"No need," Rebrov staggered out into the hallway.

Dragging Seryozha, Olga followed him out. Rebrov walked into Doc's study, grabbed on to the desk, started to push it off to the side, then coughed and spat up blood.

"What are you doing, asshole!" Olga dropped Seryozha, shoved Rebrov away, and began to push the desk herself.

Shtaube walked in, leaning forward onto two shovels. Two chisels protruded from his waistband.

"My back . . ." Seryozha wept weakly.

"Third board from the corner," Rebrov rolled onto his back. "The intermediate block, the liquid mother . . ."

Olga rushed out. Shtaube jammed the chisel into the parquet floor, pulling out a parquet block; metal flashed in the opening.

"There we go," Shtaube began to quickly rip apart the parquetry. Olga dragged in the box with the intermediate block and the suitcase with the liquid mother, then rushed over to help Shtaube. Underneath the parquetry was a large steel square held in place by eight powerful bolts. Shtaube and Olga unscrewed the bolts, plied off the steel square with chisels, and moved it off to the side. Underneath the square was a hatch sealed shut with a gate valve and a four-digit combination lock.

"Vitya!" Olga pushed Rebrov and he crawled over to the hatch.

"4242."

Shtaube entered the code, turned the handwheel, and pulled.

"Help me."

Olga grabbed on to the handwheel. The hatch opened slowly.

"Vitenka! Vitenka!" Olga threw herself onto Rebrov and kissed his pale face.

"There're steps," Shtaube looked down, "and it's dark. Those bastards had a flashlight somewhere."

"Just a minute! I remember!" Olga ran out and came back with Marik's flashlight.

"Down, down . . ." Rebrov muttered.

Olga walked down the steps into a spacious bunker, shined her flashlight around, and cried out, "it's just an empty basement!"

"Down . . ." Rebrov coughed. Shtaube dragged Seryozha over to the hatch, then Olga came back and carried him. They then lowered Rebrov, the intermediate block, and the liquid mother down through the hatch.

"The segments," Rebrov mumbled.

"Whose?" Olga and Shtaube exchanged a look.

"All of 'em."

Olga took hers and Seryozha's out of her pocket, then Shtaube took Rebrov's off of him and began to rummage through his own pockets.

"There."

Rebrov pressed his face against the concrete floor.

"Lay them out in the corners . . . in hierarchical order. The large scale in the center of the bunker . . . with the red edge on the right sides . . . all the way to the right . . ."

Olga and Shtaube walked toward the corners.

"Did they cut off my legs?" Seryozha got up onto his hands. "Where are my legs?!"

"Here, here," Shtaube muttered.

"Pull the destithread . . . through the end . . ."

"With the cross?"

"Yes."

A minute later, the destithread had been passed through all four segments. Olga pulled out the spheria and pushed it along the thread. The spheria rolled along, buzzing softly.

"Swimming . . . I don't even know . . ." Rebrov whispered, "but there . . . there's just already . . ."

"Correct it," Shtaube followed the spheria with his flashlight.

"My legs . . . my legs!" Seryozha wept, touching his bare legs in the darkness.

"They didn't pull that hard," Shtaube mumbled.

The spheria stopped.

"Vitya! What now?" Olga knelt down over the quivering spheria.

"I . . . don't exactly know . . ." Rebrov whispered.

Shtaube shined his light onto the ground beneath the spheria, touched a barely noticeable protrusion, which turned out to be a steel plate covered over in concrete. Shtaube moved the plate off to the side. Beneath the plate was a keyhole.

"The key?"

"Around . . . my neck . . ." Rebrov whispered.

Seryozha sobbed.

"The key! The key!" Olga screamed.

"Around my neck. . . . " Rebrov whispered.

She rushed over to him, felt at his neck, removed a chain with a long, flat key, and handed it to Shtaube. He put the key into the keyhole and turned it. There was a buzz, then the floor trembled and began to descend.

"We're moving, Vitya!" Olga stroked his head. Their descent through the concrete shaft was lengthy; the illuminated opening of the hatch got smaller and smaller, turned into a faint spot of light, then disappeared in the darkness. The floor stopped moving. Olga shined her flashlight around: they were surrounded by concrete walls, on one of which was a metal plaque with a keyhole. Shtaube removed the key from the hole in the floor and handed it to Olga. She inserted the key into the plaque on the wall and turned it.

A spring clicked and the plaque moved, revealing a metal indentation with a complicated surface and a multitude of holes.

"Look, Vitya!" Olga shined her light on the indentation.

Lying on the floor, Rebrov did not respond.

"Viktor Valentinych . . ." Shtaube slid over to him, "the correction."

Rebrov was silent. Shtaube turned him over onto his back. Olga shined the light on him: the slits of his eyes were motionless.

"Vitya! Vitya! Vitya!" Olga began to hit him in the face.

"I'm cold . . ." Seryozha wept.

"Hold on, I understand now," Shtaube crawled over to the box with the intermediate block, "shine it over here . . ."

Olga shifted the flashlight. Shtaube opened the box and began to undo the fastening screws.

"Ol, they hammered nails into me, Ol!" Seryozha sobbed, crawling over to her legs. "Won't you tell me, Ol? Won't you?"

"Stop it!" Olga screamed.

Seryozha sobbed, holding his hand over his mouth. Shtaube began to remove the intermediate block from the box.

"Help me . . ."

Olga helped him.

"I guessed it! The old fart figured it out!" Shtaube laughed. They brought the intermediate block to the wall and fit it into the indentation. The surface of the intermediate block lined up perfectly with the surface of the indentation. Shtaube turned the transverse-supply lever, moved the gnek to 3, turned the pole to 5, and pulled the paraclete.

"What came before 'hop' during the allotment?"

"'Pause.'"

Shtaube touched the longitudinal-feed lever. The gnek began to wrap around itself. Shtaube turned the paraclete to auto-reverse and

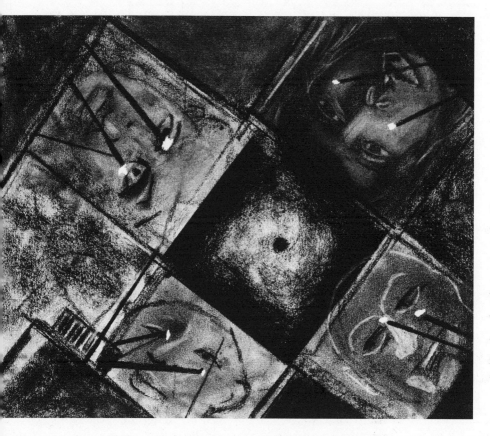

Their heads descended as they unfolded outward.

moved the pole to 7. When the red risks of the paraclete and the gnek were in alignment, he pulled the ring. There was a whistle; all of the axes sank into the nests, then the wall trembled and shifted right. As soon as it had moved all the way over, an engine began to thrum and there was a burst of light in the newly opened space. Shtaube grabbed on to the suitcase with the liquid mother and crawled forward with it. Olga dragged Seryozha and Rebrov with her. They found themselves in a spacious concrete bunker. There were four PRM-118 cutting presses in the center of the room. There was also a nickel-plated funnel fitted to the floor.

"Lord have mercy . . . Lord have mercy . . ." crossing himself, Shtaube crawled over to the funnel, grabbed on to the suitcase with the liquid mother, and began to hack at the lock on the suitcase with a chisel.

"And you wanted us to blow ourselves up!" Olga laughed nervously, then burst into tears.

"Enough, enough, my God, enough . . ." Shtaube pulled out the stopper and tilted the suitcase over. A sticky, brown fluid flowed into the funnel.

Olga took her clothes off and removed Seryozha's sweater. The boy screamed.

"Have a little patience, darling . . . no! I can't believe it! Seryozhenka! Vitya! And what if it doesn't work?! Why! Why do we have to?!" Olga sobbed.

"Enough . . . enough . . ." Shtaube dropped the empty suitcase and began to undress.

Olga picked up Seryozha and lay him down onto the bed of one of the cutting presses.

"Already, Ol?" he asked.

"Yes, darling," she placed his motionless, blue legs into the fastening grooves. "And your arms over there . . ."

Seryozha put his arms through the fastening holes.

"Please don't . . . do it too early . . ." now naked, Shtaube crawled over to Rebrov and began to untie his boot laces.

Their four hearts stopped.

"Shtaube, darling, I can't believe it!" Olga laughed, rubbing blood all over her face. "We made it!"

"Don't do it too early . . . help me . . ."

They undressed Rebrov together and lay him down onto another bed.

"There's a lever there . . ." Shtaube got into his own press.

"I know," Olga pulled the red lever on Rebrov's press, then the lever on Seryozha's press.

Shtaube reached for his own lever and pulled it.

"Quickly now . . ."

Olga rushed over to her own press, lay down, and pulled the lever. The presses began to operate. Their heads descended as they unfolded outward.

"Ol!" Seryozha cried out.

"Quiet! Quiet!" Olga wept joyfully.

"There . . ." Shtaube closed his eyes and licked at his cracked lips.

Faceted rods entered their heads, shoulders, stomachs, and legs. The incisors rotated, the pneumobatteries shifted down, the liquid freon began to flow, and the heads of the presses covered the beds. Twenty-eight minutes later, their four hearts, pressed into cubes and frozen, fell down into a roller, where they were marked up like dice. Three minutes later, the roller dropped them onto a field of ice made up of liquid mother. Their four hearts stopped.

6, 2, 5, 5.

1991

Vladimir Sorokin Vladimir Sorokin was born in a small town outside of Moscow in 1955. He trained as an engineer at the Moscow Institute of Oil and Gas, but turned to art and writing, becoming a major presence in the Moscow underground of the 1980s. His work was banned in the Soviet Union, and his first novel, *The Queue*, was published by the famed émigré dissident Andrei Sinyavsky in France in 1983. In 1992, Sorokin's *Their Four Hearts* was nominated for the Russian Booker Prize; in 1999, the publication of the controversial novel *Blue Lard*, which included a sex scene between clones of Stalin and Khrushchev, led to public demonstrations against the book and to demands that Sorokin be prosecuted as a pornographer; in 2001, he received the Andrei Bely Award for outstanding contributions to Russian literature. Sorokin is also the author of the screenplays for *Moscow*, *The Kopeck*, and *4*, and of the libretto for Leonid Desyatnikov's *The Children of Rosenthal*, the first new opera to be commissioned by the Bolshoi Theater since the 1970s. He has written numerous plays and short stories, and his work has been translated throughout the world. Among his most recent books are *Sugar Kremlin* and *Day of the Oprichnik*. He lives in Moscow.

Gregory Klassen earned his bachelor's degree at the University of Wisconsin-Oshkosh and did advanced study at Kunst Akademie Dusseldorf, Germany. He was one of the last artists to study under Gerhard Richter in the 1990s. He has exhibited at galleries and museums internationally.

Max Lawton is a translator, novelist, and musician. He received his BA in Russian Literature and Culture from Columbia University and his MPhil from Queen's College, Oxford, where he wrote a dissertation comparing Céline and Dostoevsky. He has translated many books by Vladimir Sorokin. Max is also the author of two novels currently awaiting publication and is writing his doctoral dissertation on phenomenology and the twentieth-century novel at Columbia University, where he also teaches Russian. He is a member of four noise-music ensembles.

MICHAL AJVAZ, *The Golden Age.*
The Other City.

PIERRE ALBERT-BIROT, *Grabinoulor.*

YUZ ALESHKOVSKY, *Kangaroo.*

FELIPE ALFAU, *Chromos.*
Locos.

JOE AMATO, *Samuel Taylor's Last Night.*

IVAN ÂNGELO, *The Celebration.*
The Tower of Glass.

ANTÓNIO LOBO ANTUNES, *Knowledge of Hell.*
The Splendor of Portugal.

ALAIN ARIAS-MISSON, *Theatre of Incest.*

JOHN ASHBERY & JAMES SCHUYLER, *A Nest of Ninnies.*

ROBERT ASHLEY, *Perfect Lives.*

GABRIELA AVIGUR-ROTEM, *Heatwave and Crazy Birds.*

DJUNA BARNES, *Ladies Almanack.*
Ryder.

JOHN BARTH, *Letters.*
Sabbatical.

DONALD BARTHELME, *The King.*
Paradise.

SVETISLAV BASARA, *Chinese Letter.*

MIQUEL BAUÇÀ, *The Siege in the Room.*

RENÉ BELLETTO, *Dying.*

MAREK BIENCZYK, *Transparency.*

ANDREI BITOV, *Pushkin House.*

ANDREJ BLATNIK, *You Do Understand.*
Law of Desire.

LOUIS PAUL BOON, *Chapel Road.*
My Little War.
Summer in Termuren.

ROGER BOYLAN, *Killoyle.*

IGNÁCIO DE LOYOLA BRANDÃO, *Anonymous Celebrity.*
Zero.

BONNIE BREMSER, *Troia: Mexican Memoirs.*

CHRISTINE BROOKE-ROSE, *Amalgamemnon.*

BRIGID BROPHY, *In Transit.*
The Prancing Novelist.

GERALD L. BRUNS, *Modern Poetry and the Idea of Language.*

GABRIELLE BURTON, *Heartbreak Hotel.*

MICHEL BUTOR, *Degrees.*
Mobile.

G. CABRERA INFANTE, *Infante's Inferno.*
Three Trapped Tigers.

JULIETA CAMPOS, *The Fear of Losing Eurydice.*

ANNE CARSON, *Eros the Bittersweet.*

ORLY CASTEL-BLOOM, *Dolly City.*

LOUIS-FERDINAND CÉLINE, *North.*
Conversations with Professor Y.
London Bridge.

MARIE CHAIX, *The Laurels of Lake Constance.*

HUGO CHARTERIS, *The Tide Is Right.*

ERIC CHEVILLARD, *Demolishing Nisard.*
The Author and Me.

MARC CHOLODENKO, *Mordechai Schamz.*

JOSHUA COHEN, *Witz.*

EMILY HOLMES COLEMAN, *The Shutter of Snow.*

ERIC CHEVILLARD, *The Author and Me.*

ROBERT COOVER, *A Night at the Movies.*

STANLEY CRAWFORD, *Log of the S.S. The Mrs Unguentine.*
Some Instructions to My Wife.

RENÉ CREVEL, *Putting My Foot in It.*

RALPH CUSACK, *Cadenza.*

NICHOLAS DELBANCO, *Sherbrookes.*
The Count of Concord.

NIGEL DENNIS, *Cards of Identity.*

PETER DIMOCK, *A Short Rhetoric for Leaving the Family.*

ARIEL DORFMAN, *Konfidenz.*

COLEMAN DOWELL, *Island People.*
Too Much Flesh and Jabez.

ARKADII DRAGOMOSHCHENKO, *Dust.*

RIKKI DUCORNET, *Phosphor in Dreamland.*
The Complete Butcher's Tales.

RIKKI DUCORNET (cont.), *The Jade Cabinet.*
The Fountains of Neptune.

WILLIAM EASTLAKE, *The Bamboo Bed.*
Castle Keep.
Lyric of the Circle Heart.

JEAN ECHENOZ, *Chopin's Move.*

STANLEY ELKIN, *A Bad Man.*
Criers and Kibitzers, Kibitzers and Criers.
The Dick Gibson Show.
The Franchiser.
The Living End.
Mrs. Ted Bliss.

FRANÇOIS EMMANUEL, *Invitation to a Voyage.*

PAUL EMOND, *The Dance of a Sham.*

SALVADOR ESPRIU, *Ariadne in the Grotesque Labyrinth.*

LESLIE A. FIEDLER, *Love and Death in the American Novel.*

JUAN FILLOY, *Op Oloop.*

ANDY FITCH, *Pop Poetics.*

GUSTAVE FLAUBERT, *Bouvard and Pécuchet.*

KASS FLEISHER, *Talking out of School.*

JON FOSSE, *Aliss at the Fire.*
Melancholy.

FORD MADOX FORD, *The March of Literature.*

MAX FRISCH, *I'm Not Stiller.*
Man in the Holocene.

CARLOS FUENTES, *Christopher Unborn.*
Distant Relations.
Terra Nostra.
Where the Air Is Clear.

TAKEHIKO FUKUNAGA, *Flowers of Grass.*

WILLIAM GADDIS, JR., *The Recognitions.*

JANICE GALLOWAY, *Foreign Parts.*
The Trick Is to Keep Breathing.

WILLIAM H. GASS, *Life Sentences.*
The Tunnel.
The World Within the Word.
Willie Masters' Lonesome Wife.

GÉRARD GAVARRY, *Hoppla! 1 2 3.*

ETIENNE GILSON, *The Arts of the Beautiful.*
Forms and Substances in the Arts.

C. S. GISCOMBE, *Giscome Road.*
Here.

DOUGLAS GLOVER, *Bad News of the Heart.*

WITOLD GOMBROWICZ, *A Kind of Testament.*

PAULO EMÍLIO SALES GOMES, *P's Three Women.*

GEORGI GOSPODINOV, *Natural Novel.*

JUAN GOYTISOLO, *Count Julian.*
Juan the Landless.
Makbara.
Marks of Identity.

HENRY GREEN, *Blindness.*
Concluding.
Doting.
Nothing.

JACK GREEN, *Fire the Bastards!*

JIŘÍ GRUŠA, *The Questionnaire.*

MELA HARTWIG, *Am I a Redundant Human Being?*

JOHN HAWKES, *The Passion Artist.*
Whistlejacket.

ELIZABETH HEIGHWAY, ED., *Contemporary Georgian Fiction.*

AIDAN HIGGINS, *Balcony of Europe.*
Blind Man's Bluff.
Bornholm Night-Ferry.
Langrishe, Go Down.
Scenes from a Receding Past.

KEIZO HINO, *Isle of Dreams.*

KAZUSHI HOSAKA, *Plainsong.*

ALDOUS HUXLEY, *Antic Hay.*
Point Counter Point.
Those Barren Leaves.
Time Must Have a Stop.

NAOYUKI II, *The Shadow of a Blue Cat.*

DRAGO JANČAR, *The Tree with No Name.*

MIKHEIL JAVAKHISHVILI, *Kvachi.*

GERT JONKE, *The Distant Sound.*
Homage to Czerny.
The System of Vienna.

NICHOLAS MOSLEY, *Accident.*
Assassins.
Catastrophe Practice.
A Garden of Trees.
Hopeful Monsters.
Imago Bird.
Inventing God.
Look at the Dark.
Metamorphosis.
Natalie Natalia.
Serpent.

WARREN MOTTE, *Fables of the Novel:*
French Fiction since 1990.
Fiction Now: The French Novel in the
21st Century.
Mirror Gazing.
Oulipo: A Primer of Potential Literature.

GERALD MURNANE, *Barley Patch.*
Inland.

YVES NAVARRE, *Our Share of Time.*
Sweet Tooth.

DOROTHY NELSON, *In Night's City.*
Tar and Feathers.

ESHKOL NEVO, *Homesick.*

WILFRIDO D. NOLLEDO, *But for*
the Lovers.

BORIS A. NOVAK, *The Master of*
Insomnia.

FLANN O'BRIEN, *At Swim-Two-Birds.*
The Best of Myles.
The Dalkey Archive.
The Hard Life.
The Poor Mouth.
The Third Policeman.

CLAUDE OLLIER, *The Mise-en-Scène.*
Wert and the Life Without End.

PATRIK OUŘEDNÍK, *Europeana.*
The Opportune Moment, 1855.

BORIS PAHOR, *Necropolis.*

FERNANDO DEL PASO, *News from*
the Empire.
Palinuro of Mexico.

ROBERT PINGET, *The Inquisitory.*
Mahu or The Material.
Trio.

MANUEL PUIG, *Betrayed by Rita*
Hayworth.

The Buenos Aires Affair.
Heartbreak Tango.

RAYMOND QUENEAU, *The Last Days.*
Odile.
Pierrot Mon Ami.
Saint Glinglin.

ANN QUIN, *Berg.*
Passages.
Three.
Tripticks.

ISHMAEL REED, *The Free-Lance*
Pallbearers.
The Last Days of Louisiana Red.
Ishmael Reed: The Plays.
Juice!
The Terrible Threes.
The Terrible Twos.
Yellow Back Radio Broke-Down.

JASIA REICHARDT, *15 Journeys Warsaw*
to London.

JOÃO UBALDO RIBEIRO, *House of the*
Fortunate Buddhas.

JEAN RICARDOU, *Place Names.*

RAINER MARIA RILKE,
The Notebooks of Malte Laurids Brigge.

JULIÁN RÍOS, *The House of Ulysses.*
Larva: A Midsummer Night's Babel.
Poundemonium.

ALAIN ROBBE-GRILLET, *Project for a*
Revolution in New York.
A Sentimental Novel.

AUGUSTO ROA BASTOS, *I the Supreme.*

DANIËL ROBBERECHTS, *Arriving in*
Avignon.

JEAN ROLIN, *The Explosion of the*
Radiator Hose.

OLIVIER ROLIN, *Hotel Crystal.*

ALIX CLEO ROUBAUD, *Alix's Journal.*

JACQUES ROUBAUD, *The Form of*
a City Changes Faster, Alas, Than the
Human Heart.
The Great Fire of London.
Hortense in Exile.
Hortense Is Abducted.
Mathematics: The Plurality of Worlds of
Lewis.
Some Thing Black.

RAYMOND ROUSSEL, *Impressions of Africa.*

VEDRANA RUDAN, *Night.*

PABLO M. RUIZ, *Four Cold Chapters on the Possibility of Literature.*

GERMAN SADULAEV, *The Maya Pill.*

TOMAŽ ŠALAMUN, *Soy Realidad.*

LYDIE SALVAYRE, *The Company of Ghosts.*
The Lecture.
The Power of Flies.

LUIS RAFAEL SÁNCHEZ, *Macho Camacho's Beat.*

SEVERO SARDUY, *Cobra & Maitreya.*

NATHALIE SARRAUTE, *Do You Hear Them?*
Martereau.
The Planetarium.

STIG SÆTERBAKKEN, *Siamese.*
Self-Control.
Through the Night.

ARNO SCHMIDT, *Collected Novellas.*
Collected Stories.
Nobodaddy's Children.
Two Novels.

ASAF SCHURR, *Motti.*

GAIL SCOTT, *My Paris.*

DAMION SEARLS, *What We Were Doing and Where We Were Going.*

JUNE AKERS SEESE,
Is This What Other Women Feel Too?

BERNARD SHARE, *Inish.*
Transit.

VIKTOR SHKLOVSKY, *Bowstring.*
Literature and Cinematography.
Theory of Prose.
Third Factory.
Zoo, or Letters Not about Love.

PIERRE SINIAC, *The Collaborators.*

KJERSTI A. SKOMSVOLD,
The Faster I Walk, the Smaller I Am.

JOSEF ŠKVORECKÝ, *The Engineer of Human Souls.*

GILBERT SORRENTINO, *Aberration of Starlight.*
Blue Pastoral.
Crystal Vision.

Imaginative Qualities of Actual Things.
Mulligan Stew. Red the Fiend.
Steelwork.
Under the Shadow.

MARKO SOSIČ, *Ballerina, Ballerina.*

ANDRZEJ STASIUK, *Dukla.*
Fado.

GERTRUDE STEIN, *The Making of Americans.*
A Novel of Thank You.

LARS SVENDSEN, *A Philosophy of Evil.*

PIOTR SZEWC, *Annihilation.*

GONÇALO M. TAVARES, *A Man: Klaus Klump.*
Jerusalem.
Learning to Pray in the Age of Technique.

LUCIAN DAN TEODOROVICI,
Our Circus Presents . . .

NIKANOR TERATOLOGEN, *Assisted Living.*

STEFAN THEMERSON, *Hobson's Island.*
The Mystery of the Sardine.
Tom Harris.

TAEKO TOMIOKA, *Building Waves.*

JOHN TOOMEY, *Sleepwalker.*

DUMITRU TSEPENEAG, *Hotel Europa.*
The Necessary Marriage.
Pigeon Post.
Vain Art of the Fugue.

ESTHER TUSQUETS, *Stranded.*

DUBRAVKA UGRESIC, *Lend Me Your Character.*
Thank You for Not Reading.

TOR ULVEN, *Replacement.*

MATI UNT, *Brecht at Night.*
Diary of a Blood Donor.
Things in the Night.

ÁLVARO URIBE & OLIVIA SEARS, EDS.,
Best of Contemporary Mexican Fiction.

ELOY URROZ, *Friction.*
The Obstacles.

LUISA VALENZUELA, *Dark Desires and the Others.*
He Who Searches.

PAUL VERHAEGHEN, *Omega Minor.*

BORIS VIAN, *Heartsnatcher.*

LLORENÇ VILLALONGA, *The Dolls'
Room.*

TOOMAS VINT, *An Unending Landscape.*

ORNELA VORPSI, *The Country Where No
One Ever Dies.*

AUSTRYN WAINHOUSE, *Hedyphagetica.*

CURTIS WHITE, *America's Magic
Mountain.*
The Idea of Home.
Memories of My Father Watching TV.
Requiem.

DIANE WILLIAMS,
Excitability: Selected Stories.
Romancer Erector.

DOUGLAS WOOLF, *Wall to Wall.*
Ya! & John-Juan.

JAY WRIGHT, *Polynomials and Pollen.*
The Presentable Art of Reading Absence.

PHILIP WYLIE, *Generation of Vipers.*

MARGUERITE YOUNG, *Angel in the
Forest.*
Miss MacIntosh, My Darling.

REYOUNG, *Unbabbling.*

VLADO ŽABOT, *The Succubus.*

ZORAN ŽIVKOVIĆ , *Hidden Camera.*

LOUIS ZUKOFSKY, *Collected Fiction.*

VITOMIL ZUPAN, *Minuet for Guitar.*

SCOTT ZWIREN, *God Head.*

AND MORE . . .